## Praise for
# Kristine Kathryn Rusch

"Rusch is a great storyteller."

—*RT Book Reviews*

"Whether [Rusch] writes high fantasy, horror, sf, or contemporary fantasy, I've always been fascinated by her ability to tell a story with that enviable gift of invisible prose. She's one of those very few writers whose style takes me right into the story—the words and pages disappear as the characters and their story swallows me whole….Rusch has style."

—Charles de Lint

"A masterful writer is at work."

—Orson Scott Card
*New York Times* bestselling author

"Rusch's greatest strength…is her ability to close down a story and leave the reader feeling that the author could not possibly have wrung any more satisfaction out of the piece."

—*The Kansas City Star*

"Rusch is a great storyteller—easily the equal of Patterson or Koontz."

—*Analog*

"Kristine Kathryn Rusch is one of the best writers in the field."

"[Rusch's] writing style is simple but elegant, and her characterization excellent."

"Like early Ray Bradbury, Rusch has the ability to switch on a universal dark."

"Kristine Kathryn Rusch's crime stories are exceptional, both in plot and in style."

"[Rusch's] short fiction is golden."

## Praise for the Retrieval Artist series

"If you love puzzle mysteries, crime novels, well-invented sci-fi worlds, or stories about characters you can believe in and care about, you owe it to yourself to give Rusch's Retrieval Artist novels a try."

"What links [Miles Flint] to his most memorable literary ancestors is his hard-won ability to perceive the complex nature of morality and live with the burden of his own inevitable failure."

*—Locus*

## Praise for the Smokey Dalton series
### (writing as Kris Nelscott)

"Nelscott's series setting, in the turbulent late '60s, gives her books layers of issues of racism, class, and war, all of which still seem to remain sadly timely today."

*—Oregonian*

"Nelscott has her own, very distinct voice, and her series creates its own deeply satisfying pleasures and cogent points."

*—Seattle Times*

"It's not hard to draw parallels between Nelscott's PI Smokey Dalton and Walter Mosley's Easy Rawlins, another secretive, canny black man trying to solve mysteries while circumspectly navigating the white world. But Dalton's no knock-off. (Would you label the hundreds of hard-boiled detectives who've appeared in Raymond Chandler's wake mere Marlow Xeroxes because they're white?)"

*—Entertainment Weekly*

# Also by
# Kristine Kathryn Rusch

## The Retrieval Artist Series:

*The Disappeared*
*Extremes*
*Consequences*
*Buried Deep*
*Paloma*
*Recovery Man*
*Duplicate Effort*
*Anniversary Day*
*Blowback*

## The Smokey Dalton Series (as Kris Nelscott):

*A Dangerous Road*
*Smoke-Filled Rooms*
*Thin Walls*
*Stone Cribs*
*War at Home*
*Days of Rage*

# FIVE FOR THE WINTER HOLIDAYS

## KRISTINE KATHRYN RUSCH

WMG
Publishing

# Five for the Winter Holidays

"Pudgygate" by Kristine Kathryn Rusch first published in *Cat Crimes Takes A Vacation*, edited by Ed Gorman & Martin H. Greenberg, Donald I Fine, 1995.

"Loop" by Kristine Kathryn Rusch first published in *VB Tech Journal*, November, 1995.

"Boz" by Kristine Kathryn Rusch first published on the SciFi.com website, December 23, 2005.

"Disaster Relief," by Kristine Kathryn Rusch first published in *Wizards Inc.*, edited by Martin H. Greenberg and Loren L. Coleman, Daw Books, November 2007.

"Millennium Babies" by Kristine Kathryn Rusch first published in *Asimov's Science Fiction Magazine*, January, 2000.

## WMG Publishing
www.wmgpublishing.com

# Contents

# FIVE FOR THE WINTER HOLIDAYS

## KRISTINE KATHRYN RUSCH

# Introduction

*M*Y FAVORITE HOLIDAY IS HALLOWEEN. Yet it doesn't inspire me to write a lot of stories. I write a lot of Christmas stories, maybe because I read a lot of them. I think Charles Dickens started me on that tradition. Christmas stories have a trajectory, and some expectations to go with them. Generally they're upbeat and heartwarming.

But other holiday stories don't carry such expectations. Still, I'll give you a spoiler here: nothing in this collection will upset you. No horror stories. No bloody murder stories. Just five stories that have their origins in the winter holidays.

Not all of the stories take place on those holidays. Take, for example, "Pudgygate." I initially wrote that story for an anthology of cat crimes. The fact that it centers around a traditional Thanksgiving meal held in an English manor house with royalty present just shows how twisted my mind gets.

The story is dedicated to the inspiration for the tale: Thorn B., who adored turkey. He was a little white cat, who got into trouble every single Thanksgiving. We always hold a large celebration here, with anywhere from five to thirty guests. The cats consider themselves part of the celebration as well, and many of our Thanksgiving stories surround rather spectacular thefts of the feline kind.

A cat makes another appearance in "Disaster Relief." Ruby is a reoccurring character in my fiction, along with her human, Winston. "Disaster Relief" begins the day after Christmas, 2004, and was inspired by that awful year, 2005. Like "Pudgygate," "Disaster Relief" isn't really about the holiday so much as the holiday spirit.

The other story not really about the holiday but inspired by it is "Millennium Babies." A news piece inspired the story. The contests to find the first baby of the millennium actually happened—but not in the real beginning of the millennium. As the story mentions, the contests were held for the first babies of the year 2000. The millennium didn't begin until 2001. Details, details. The story won a Hugo, science fiction's most prestigious award.

The other two stories in this volume are Christmas stories. One, "Boz," is set in the far future. The other, "Loop," is set in the near future. Both look at holiday traditions in a somewhat different way.

Five stories, which should give you something to read for four holidays. You can read "Pudgygate" on Thanksgiving, "Loop" and "Boz" around Christmas, "Disaster Relief" on Boxing Day, and "Millennium Babies" on New Year's Day. Eventually, I'll have a few Halloween stories, and maybe a Fourth of July story. But for now, these five stories will have to do for your holiday fix. Enjoy!

*—Kristine Kathryn Rusch*
*Lincoln City, Oregon*
*November 21, 2010*

# Pudgygate

THE WIND OFF THE PACIFIC OCEAN IS COLD, even in Malibu. A group of fifteen young men huddle close to the celebratory bonfire they have built on a secluded stretch of beach. A short distance away, the cars wait like obedient children. Inside one, a cellular phone rings for the fifth time in an hour.

The sand is still warm from the day's sun. A tapped keg topples like a drunken soldier, but few of the men are drinking any more. They have been talking since noon, catching up on the years since they graduated from Cal Tech and went on their separate ways.

The conversation has deteriorated from highly placed and sometimes top secret research, grant applications, and the possibility of full professorships (as opposed to careers in government science labs) to the kinds of conversations they used to have in the dorm lounges late at night.

Desmond brought up his most embarrassing moment—something to do with toilet paper and the girl's locker room when he was in Middle School—and Benjamin followed with his, Scott with his, and Michael with his.

But the conversation has stopped, for Reuben has taken the stage. Reuben, who took a mysterious trip to London in his senior year, and has refused to talk about it ever since. Reuben is a kind of hero to them all because he crammed two semesters into one that last year, and still managed to graduate with honors.

"Toilet paper on your shoes?" he says as he settles in the center of the circle, legs crossed. He looks like the before picture in a body-building ad, but his skin has cleared in the intervening years, giving him a handsomeness he never possessed before. His hair is longer too, just touching the tips of his tiny ears. "Getting caught peeing on your coach's Volvo? Throwing up all over the Homecoming Queen at the dance? Come on, men, that's kid stuff."

"Kid stuff?" says Scott. His tone is a bit defensive. His Homecoming Queen story did get a lot of laughs.

"Yeah," Reuben says. "Kid stuff. My most embarrassing moment happened at a state dinner when I was in England." And then, because the group does not gasp or do anything else to show that it is impressed, he adds, "In front of Princess Di."

"Princess Di?" asks Benjamin. "*The* Princess Di?"

"Man," says a voice in the blackness. "She's hot. Old, but hot."

"You didn't get sick on her, did you?" asks Scott.

"Not quite," says Reuben, "but it might have been better if I did."

\*\*\*

WHEN LESTER ASKED ME if I wanted to meet Princess Di (Reuben says, settling into the story-telling cadence he is known for within the group), I never thought it through. I knew Lester had connections—his father was an MP (that's Member of Parliament for you non-anglophiles)—and Lester himself had spent summers with the Royal Family. So I spent my last thousand bucks and skipped the first semester of my final year at Cal Tech to winter in London.

I had brought a tux and my best hair cream. I even thought of getting my nose pierced, but then a friend told me that Di was not an Xer and might find the entire idea a bit gross. (I was a bit relieved; I am prone to sinus infections.)

That same friend sniffed at me for even imagining that anything would come of my meeting with Di. After all, she was a princess and I was a scrawny physics student who knew his way around quarks and computer languages—not the elegant dining rooms of Europe. But I had watched *Pretty Woman* enough to learn about place settings—

("*Pretty Woman*?" Scott says. "You watched *Pretty Woman* more than once?"

("Leave him alone," says Benjamin. "It was a date movie. You did see it on dates, didn't you?")

—and I figured what I didn't know, Lester would teach me.

And teach me he did. Place settings, Waterford crystal, the order of all seven courses. Seems Di had cut back on her social engagements. Lester's family was one of the few receiving her, and while I stayed at the house, I learned not to answer the phone which rang incessantly, particularly in the middle of the night.

This was before the press learned that one of Di's quirks was her penchant for phone harassment. Before the world learned that Di slept with her riding instructor and Charles never loved her. But it was after the bulimia stories, Squidgygate, and the public separation.

Di was lonely.

I hoped to take advantage of that.

Until Lester told me the real reason he had asked me to spend September with his family. They had to host a minor state dinner with the head of state of a small country in the middle of Europe. The Head of State, like the rest of us mortals, was fascinated with Shy Di, and refused to meet with John Major unless he could also meet with Diana. A ticklish thing at best, since at that point, Di was on the farthest outs she could be with the Royals. They refused to socialize with her, and so Lester's father offered, in June, to host the dinner privately.

No one could have known how difficult private had become.

You see, Di was a darling of the international press, and the center of tabloid attention at home. If she wasn't so frail, she probably would have killed a reporter or two by then. The family learned, in July, that hiring a catering staff was out of the question. Half the reporters on Fleet Street now moonlighted for the bigger name restaurants in hopes of a story. So the family had to rely on people they trusted, and when they came up one waiter short, Lester thought of me.

And all those posters of Di in my dorm room.

He figured I was an easy mark. He was right.

(Except for the screaming match the morning I found out. I slammed out of the house, stopped on that quiet English street, with its lovely row of trees, and realized that it was my pride or a chance to gaze on Di in person. I, of course, turned around.)

So, on the night in question, when I should have been wearing my silver tux with my grandfather's diamond cufflinks, I was, instead, wearing a borrowed black tux stained with gravy. The tastefully tight cummerbund covered the gravy stain, but not the feeling of shoddiness it imparted in me. And I still couldn't learn when to serve from the left, and when to serve from the right.

Lester, in exasperation, finally gave up, told me to watch the other waiters—most of whom were as pimply, scrawny and underfed as myself—then retired to his own room to dress for dinner.

Lester would get to eat with the family.

The traitor.

\*\*\*

THE CHEF WAS REALLY THE GARDENER, a middle-aged Idahonian named (I kid you not) Bubba. Bubba was big, Bubba was strong, and Bubba could protect a princess. But Bubba had only one seven course meal in his rather limited repertoire—a traditional Thanksgiving dinner with all the trimmings. The Americans among the wait staff recognized it and tittered when they realized they were serving a colonial meal to the imperialists. But Bubba took offense at that.

"Them pilgrim guys," he said more than once, "was Brits when they landed on that Rock."

We all agreed, but took a vow of silence anyway. To us, a turkey dinner could never be elegant, not even when it was served on the family's highly polished serving set. And all of us worried, in one way or another, what that infatuated Head of State would think when faced with drumsticks, yams and pumpkin pie.

"Not our problem," said Cletus, the blond All-American hunk who had gone to MIT with Lester during his one summer in Boston. If Di noticed anyone on the wait staff, it would be Cletus.

"Nope. We just gotta make sure we serve this stuff in the best possible way," said Finigan, the tall skinny redhead who had met Lester during that infamous year at the University of Chicago.

"I hope you guys know what goes left and what goes right," I said. I was so nervous my face had broken out in four different places.

"Pay it no never mind," said Bobby Ray, the short, square Louisiana boy who had introduced Lester to Bourbon Street during his brief (and no longer recorded on his transcript) stay at Tulane. "If one of us messes up, all of us mess up. It might be an ice breaker."

"Lester's mother said we weren't to speak to the guests," said Percival, the pasty twenty-five-year old who had yet to reach his adult growth. He had been the class goat, and Lester's bunkmate at Eton during the period Lester called "the hell years."

"Lester's mother," said Georgia, the only girl in the group, with a decided sneer. Georgia was a gum-chewing Angelino of Puerto Rican descent whose black hair was so short, and body was so thin she looked better dressed as a man than all of us except Cletus. "Lester's mother's spine is so straight that she can't bend over to save her life."

Did I say that Georgia predates Lester's Cal Tech period by a wild twenty-four hours that ended in a fight outside the Viper Room? And this time, Lester was not the one caught fighting.

"First course," Bubba said.

We all turned and froze in horror. Dozens of deviled eggs stared up from the shiny silver serving trays like glow-in-the-dark eyeballs.

"These are the appetizers?" Percival asked, his voice small.

"You gotta problem with that?" Bubba crossed his thick arms—his wrists alone were the size of Percival's skull—and frowned.

"Absolutely not," Percival said with more pluck than I had given him credit for. He picked up the first tray, balanced it on his shoulder like a good waiter, and backed out of the swinging door.

As he backed out of the door, Lester's neutered tom, Pudge, sauntered in. Pudge was square as a linebacker, white with a touch of red, and had blue eyes from a roaming Siamese in his family's past. He was also the most focused cat on the planet.

None of us thought much about him, though, since he had never focused on any of us.

Until the salad course.

\*\*\*

THOSE OF YOU WHO KNOW LESTER should be aware that this was happening in the London Townhouse, not in the 18th century manse in Cheswick or the family estate outside of Kent. For those of you who don't know Lester— well, bear with me a moment while I set the scene.

The brownstone had been remodeled in the recent past by an architect with Vision. The kitchen—which was large enough to seat all of Parliament and still allow someone to cook a meal—was now off the formal dining room. Family dining was down the hall.

"Inconvenience every day of the week except Sunday," Lester liked to say.

Formal dining was a room as large as the kitchen, filled with heavy mahogany furniture, and two chandeliers that looked as if they had once been made for gaslight. A Chinese screen (from some aunt's missionary days) hid the wet bar in the corner. Objets d'art lined the shelves on the walls—collectible plates (which Lester assured me *were not* limited editions from the Franklin Mint), antique vases (pronounced vaaaaazes), and chipped, ugly statutes from some uncle's Egyptian salad days. (At the other formal meal I attended, the guy from the British Museum drooled over those damaged things and claimed that the family might want to do a public service and donate the statues, particularly the one of Horus which even I knew was worth something because it had rubies instead of eyes. Nothing more was said. Public service, apparently, is not Lester's family's forte.)

The guests mingled in the library which Lester's parents had settled on after a heated debate ("The front parlor has your family's hideous weapons collection," snapped Lester's mother, "which is not something a young woman in the middle of a marital crisis should see, or have access to, for that matter!") and sipped expensive liquor while Bubba finished the first course.

We were to put the appetizers on the table, and then the butler would call the family into dinner. We tried to arrange the serving platters of eggs as far away from the lights as possible, but the butler (who had been with the family nearly fifty years) still blanched. Nonetheless, he went off to perform his duty, and we fled the room.

In the kitchen, Pudge sat in front of the hot stove, staring at the roasting turkey inside. Bubba was preparing the second course—the soup course—for which (it soon became apparent) he had special-ordered a case of Campbell's Chicken Noodle from the States. The sound of the can opener didn't arouse Pudge who was more intent on the sizzling bird than even the opportunity for cat food.

We had ten minutes to debate the best serving method for soup while Bubba zapped individual bowls in the microwave. ("Are you supposed to do that with fine china?" Georgia asked. "You seen anything else I should use?" Bubba countered.) He topped each boiling bowlful with a sprig of parsley then sent us on our way.

The soup course allowed us to get our first glimpse of the guests.

The foreign Head of State (whom we were to refer to as Your Honored and Respected Sir, if we were to refer at all) wore a dark gray tux that accented his silvering hair. His face, unlined thanks to some obvious plastic surgery, had all the warmth of the Tower of London. His wife, wearing a gown covered with tiny diamonds, looked like an aging Barbie doll. Lester's family filled the gaps in the table. And Di, even though she was surrounded by a crowd of people, sat alone.

She wore a tiny tiara in her hair that matched the choker around her neck. Her dress was off the shoulder, revealing the slight rise of her breasts. She smiled as she flirted with the Head of State, but the smile never reached her eyes. Her voice had an airy, little girlish tone that I hadn't noticed in her public speeches. She ate part of an egg, leaving a dainty half-moon on her plate.

I whisked the plate away. Wonder of wonders, miracle of miracles, I had been assigned to Di's chair. Lester winked at me as I whisked with one hand, and set with the other.

Di's hair smelled of jasmine, and I bent so close to her I could feel the warmth of her skin.

I managed to place the soup bowl without spilling a drop.

Di didn't even notice.

And then, all too soon, it was over. We carried the dirty dishes back to the kitchen (to be dealt with by the morning's cleaning crew), and to await our next task.

Cletus went to the window to count the bodyguards the Princess had brought with her. Finigan went to the other window to see if he could tell the Princess's guards from the foreign head's of state. Georgia kibitzed from the back, betting they couldn't tell the Lester's family guards from the guest's guards.

I sat on a chair near the stove, which put me right next to Pudge. He was still staring at the turkey, his big blue eyes shining with fascination.

He had been at the stare-down over an hour now, and showed no signs of moving.

Bubba, on the other hand, was circling the kitchen like a man possessed. He was finally in his element. The salad course featured greens from his garden, topped with all sorts of veggies Great and Small. The veggies were nurtured by Bubba's large, but capable hands, and he treated them like precious children as he put the finishing touches on the plates.

For once, a dish I would be proud to serve to a Princess. The salad looked like something out of a restaurant, with onions sliced so thin they looked like tiny bracelets resting on top of the romaine.

The dressing boats were on the table (I had already checked when I saw Bubba and learned there was going to be a salad course), so we had nothing to worry about.

"Hey, Bubs," Georgia said. "What comes next after the salad?"

Bubba set the last plate on a tray and then grabbed potholders. "Not sure," he said. "Been thinking maybe the cranberries can be a course all by themselves."

"You're not certain?" Percival asked, his face going whiter than the butler's had when he saw the eggs. "Good God, man, this is a state dinner!"

"What do you care?" Gently, with a booted foot, Bubba shoved Pudge aside, and opened the oven door. The rich smell of roast turkey filled the kitchen. Pudge stood and approached the open door.

"Why, sir," Percival said, "I care because we, the wait staff, will have to suffer the displeasure of the guests should the meal not be, how should I say it, up to snuff."

"He means if they don't like it, we get all the flak," Bobby Ray said.

"I know what he means." Bubba pushed Pudge aside again. Then Bubba bent at the waist and hauled the turkey out of the oven. The bird was huge, golden brown, and the juices dripped from its sides into the pan below.

Bubba might not know how to cook soup, but he sure knew his turkey.

He put the turkey on the counter near the sink, then grabbed the pots filled with potatoes, and placed them on the stovetop. Then he opened the refrigerator and pulled out six pies. The fillings were loose, but I recognized them anyway: pumpkin, mincemeat, and apple. He put those in the now-empty oven.

"You can bake them all at the same temperature?" I asked.

"What is everybody, a critic?" Bubba snapped. "You try cooking a meal for the Princess a Wales. At least you guys geta look at her."

Georgia left her spot at the window and came into the kitchen. She took a piece of romaine off the nearest salad.

"Now, now, Bubba," she said, sounding not at all reassuring. "We simply want this meal to go as well as you do."

"I been working on this for the last week and—dang!" Bubba slapped a meaty hand against his own forehead. "Babe, can you open the cranberries? And kid —" he was looking at me "— I need you ta take the bread outta that fancy warming pan thing."

It took me a moment to locate the fancy warming pan thing, which proved a nice distraction so that neither Bubba or Georgia saw me grin while she harangued him for calling her Babe. I took the bread out, and arranged the slices in the wicker baskets that Bubba had left near the warming pan thing (which looked, in case you're wondering, like a giant metal bread box with a heater).

By the time I turned around, Georgia was opening large cans of imported cranberry jelly (the flat kind that takes the form of the can), Bubba was putting shredded Parmesan on the salad, and Pudge on the counter beside the turkey, happily nibbling the knobby end of a drumstick.

"Pudge!" I screamed from across the room. Bubba whirled, but Percival beat him to the cat's side. Pudge got tossed halfway across the kitchen, and slid on the tiled floor before he could skid to a stop near the back door. Cletus opened the door and tried to toss Pudge out, but a burly guard blocked the way.

"So sorry," the guard said. "No one leaves."

"Not me," Cletus said. "The cat."

"Right-o," the guard said, shrugging a bit. "Fraid I do have my orders. You never know what that cat could be concealing on his person."

"Half the princess's turkey," Finigan said.

"What?" the guard said.

"Nothing." Cletus slammed the door closed. Pudge hung from his arms, square body extended, all limbs pointing toward the turkey. His little jaw was still working its last bite and his pale blue eyes were still focused on the bird, now all the way across the room.

"Great," Finigan said. "Now what do we do with him?"

"We must serve the salad," Percival said. "It's past time."

"Yeah," Georgia muttered. "We don't want to leave them alone with that soup too long."

Bubba glared at her, but she pretended not to notice. Bobby Ray peered at the gnawed drumstick. "He only took the skin off the edge. If we peel all the skin away from that part of the bone no one will notice."

"Get out of here. You're distracting me," Bubba said.

"What about Pudge?" Cletus asked.

"Cat won't get past me a second time." Bubba literally snarled the words. He spoke with such force, I actually looked around to see if there was a cleaver handy, and sighed with relief when there wasn't.

"Okay," Cletus said. He put Pudge down. The cat zoomed like a smart missile for the turkey.

"You're covered with hair!" Georgia said, and it was true. White cat hair coated the front of Cletus's tux.

"We're exceedingly late," Percival said. "The butler just gave us A Look through the door."

"No one'll notice the hair in the dim lighting," Finigan said. "Let's go."

We grabbed our salad trays and hurried into the dining room. The soup bowls were empty. As I whisked Di's away, and replaced it with her salad plate (another lovely, deft, almost professional maneuver which she didn't notice), I overheard the Head of State's wife ask if she could get the chef's soup recipe.

Georgia snorted and Lester glared at her. "Sorry, ma'am," said Bobby Ray, who was responsible for the wife's eating enjoyment. "Closely guarded family secret."

And we all managed to stumble into the kitchen before collapsing with the giggles.

\*\*\*

In the kitchen, Bubba was making gravy. Sweat beaded on his forehead and he bit his lower lip with the concentration of a man taking the SAT test. He was swaying back and forth as if stirring made him dizzy.

The turkey cooled on the counter, Pudge-less.

It wasn't until I got all the way inside the room that I understood.

Bubba was standing on one booted foot. With the other, he was blocking Pudge who was trying to get into proper position to jump onto the counter. Much of the floor was spattered with gravy, and Pudge's whiskers had some suspicious smudges.

"Someone get that cat," Bubba said. "He don't even want no gravy. Not while that turkey's in the room."

"Give him the heart," Georgia said. "That should keep him busy for a while."

"Good idea," Cletus said.

"You do it," Bubba said. "If I stop now, we're gonna get lumps."

Cletus pulled the heart, neck, and liver from their places on the turkey's side. Each movement he made left little white cat hairs all over the counter.

"Yuck," Finigan said. "Did you do that to Lester's mother's salad?"

"Sure hope so," Cletus said with a grin.

Percival had taken over blocking duties from Bubba. For each move that Percival made, Pudge made a new one, never taking his steely-eyed gaze from the turkey. From my perspective, it looked as if Pudge and Percival were involved in a ritual dance.

Finally Cletus finished carving Pudge's meal. He waved the plate under the cat's nose—

("Hey!" Bubba shouted. "That was one of my dessert plates!")

—and then carried the plate to the back door. Pudge followed, tail high, looking as proud as if he had bagged the bird himself.

"I've been thinking," Georgia said, "that we should serve the turkey and fixings as one course, and dessert as the final course."

"That's only five," Bubba said, still stirring. "I was supposed ta do seven."

"I don't think anyone will miss the other two," Georgia said.

"What were you planning to serve after the, ah, cranberry course?" Percival asked.

"The bread course, what else?" Bubba wiped his forehead with the back of his left hand, revealing a sweat stain the size of California in his armpit.

"What else?" Georgia mouthed behind his back.

"Sounds good," Cletus said as he walked away from Pudge. The cat was gobbling his food so fast we could hear the sucking sounds across the room. "But I wanna go home sometime tonight. How about we just do what Georgia said. I'm sure they're not gonna mind either. I mean, how long would you want to spend with Lester's mom?"

"Good point," Bubba said. He pulled the gravy off the burner. "Don't make no difference to me. If anyone asks, I'll just say you guys dropped the other two courses."

"Should we break some plates as a cover?" Bobby Ray asked.

"Lord, no!" Percival said. "Do you know how much these dishes are worth?"

"It was a joke, Percy," I said, unable to take the strain any longer. In two contacts, Di hadn't even looked at me. I didn't know how to get her attention without making a fool of myself. And I was getting tired of standing in this kitchen.

"Okay," Bubba said. "You guys go clear the salad and put out dinner plates. By the time you get back, I'll have everything in their proper serving stuff."

We did as we were told. Out in the formal dining room, the conversation had turned to future of the monarchy, and Lester's father was desperately trying to turn it to something else. Di looked as if she were going to cry at any moment.

She hadn't touched her salad.

I whisked the plate away and replaced it with a larger piece of the family china.

"What is this?" Lester's mother whispered loudly to Cletus. "The invisible course?"

The butler, who was pretending to supervise, placed his hands behind his back and walked toward the table. Percival glanced in the butler's direction, and stammered, "Ah, we-we-we are br-br-bringing the main course now, ma'am."

I didn't have long to ponder what childhood memories the butler's approach raised in Percival because Di put her cool fingers on my arm. I glanced down at her manicured hand, resting so softly on my naked wrist, and I thought I had died and gone to heaven.

"Would you be so kind as to bring me a spot of tea? I do know it's out of order, but I would be ever so grateful."

Ah, gratitude. A man always likes that in a woman. It might lead her to…express it. "Certainly, your Highness," I said, and cringed as I mimicked her accent.

("Is that the embarrassing moment?" Scott asks, his sneer ready.

("No," Reuben says crossly.

("Good," Scott says. "Because if it is, make up something better, okay?")

She didn't even notice. She returned to the discussion of the monarchy by saying that she was concerned for William and Harry's future. I didn't get to hear the rest of the thought as we carried the dirty dishes into the kitchen. A huge stack of expensive but filthy china stood on the counter above the family's American-style dishwasher.

"Ain't none of them ate their salad?" Bubba asked with obvious disappointment.

"Too pretty to touch," I said, taking pity.

No one could say that about the rest of the meal. The turkey was piled haphazardly on the platters ("Didn't anyone ever show you the old one platter for white, one platter for dark routine?" Georgia asked). The potatoes looked like the snow cap on Mount Shasta. The cranberries were standing in perfect, wiggly can-shaped circles on their plates ("My mom used to at least slice it," Finigan said as he picked up the cranberry dishes and put them on the tray). And the yams looked like wizened overcooked tubers in the center of perfectly white bowls (but then they always looked like that to me). There were no garden veggies because Bubba had used them all for the salads.

And to make matters worse, no one had remembered to put on water for tea.

Bubba promised to do so while we delivered the food. I hoped he would remember. He had to deal with the turkey carcass first. Pudge was done with his little dinner and it obviously had not been enough.

"Land Shark," Cletus said, looking at the white cat circling Bubba's legs.

"Food's getting cold," Bubba said.

"The tea's for the Princess," I said again, just in case he forgot.

"Ain't it always?" Bubba muttered.

I got the turkey platters on my large server's tray and led the charge into the dining room. "Your tea is coming, Your Highness," I said as I set a platter next to Di.

She smiled at me and I felt the look all the way to my toes. I didn't even notice when the lights went out, thinking in my dazed state that the world had simply gone dark with the force of my joy.

Lester's mother screamed. His father shouted something about getting the torch (I sure hoped that was a flashlight), and the Head of State whistled for his personal body guard. Behind me came the sound of breaking glass. Bubba was yelling in the kitchen, and the swinging door slammed into the wall. I felt a rush of wind as something flew past me. I set the platter down quickly so I wouldn't drop it on Di. She had made not a sound.

"Get it off me! Get it off, I say!" quavered a querulous male voice that I didn't recognize.

The thin beam of a flashlight revealed a mess at the table. The Head of State and his wife were quivering at the far wall. Di was sitting rigidly. Lester was running out of the room—for the bodyguards I hoped—and the wait staff was frozen in mid-service.

The butler was screaming and groping with his right hand at a furry white thing braced on his shoulder. Pudge whipped his little head around. He had overshot his target, but now, with the aid of the light, he saw his quarry.

The turkey platters.

He launched himself at the table.

Lester's father brought his hand up to protect his face, lost his grip on the light, and it crashed to floor, placing us in darkness again.

Part of my brain registered the oddness of the butler's movements. Why fight a determined cat with one hand? Then the breaking glass registered.

"The butler did it!" I shouted, and ran for him. Amazingly, I reached him, grabbed him, and held him long enough for Lester's father to recover the light.

The circle of light waved around the room. In the front of the house, the bodyguards pounded on the door.

Bubba was still shouting in the kitchen, accompanied by more breaking glass. The butler was struggling, and I could barely hold him. Cletus and Bobby Ray hurried to my side as the beam of light caught the butler's left hand.

He was holding the statue of Horus, the one with the ruby eyes.

"Cedric!" said Lester's father. "Whatever are you doing?"

"It fell, sir," the butler said.

Cletus and Bobby Ray grabbed the butler's arms.

"Yeah," I said. "It fell after he broke the glass."

"Good heavens," said Lester's mother as the flashlight beam wavered and went out.

"Lester!" said his father. "Didn't you replace the batteries?"

They argued for a few minutes, the front and back doors crashed in simultaneously, and then the chandeliers came back on. "The pies!" Bubba wailed.

The Head of State and his wife were still cowering in the corner. Lester was standing beside the butler, holding the man's collar like a bounty hunter, Cletus and Bobby Ray holding him for real. The rest of the wait staff still retained their various positions.

"Pudge!" Lester's mother said, her tone revealing her shock at this newest horror.

We all looked at the cat. He was standing in the potatoes, and leaning over the turkey platter. A piece of white meat dangled from his dainty, overworked mouth.

Tears rolled down Diana's face, and she was shaking. I wanted to put a hand on her shoulder to comfort her, but couldn't.

"Your Highness, are you all right?" Lester's father asked.

Diana nodded, then burst into a gale of laughter. "I haven't had this much fun," she managed between chuckles, "since I quit teaching kindergarten."

\*\*\*

THE FIRE IS BURNING LOW. The ocean rumbles behind them. Benjamin throws the last log onto the pyre.

"I don't get it," Michael says. "The butler did what?"

"He was trying to steal the Egyptian art," Scott says.

"But why?" Michael says. "He had plenty of time to do that during the day."

Reuben shakes his head. "That's what we all thought, but it actually makes a curious kind of sense. You see, any theft would be traced back to him. But he figured on that night any disturbance would be credited to the press following Princess Di. He had drugged the coffee for the guards in the sitting room and library, and had already lifted some small items from those rooms. He also did some damage to the furniture to make it look like the losses were breakage. By the time the thefts were discovered, he planned to have sold the pieces to some black marketeers, and to be long gone."

"I thought you said only trusted servants were on that night," someone says from the darkness in the back.

"Well," Reuben says, "he had been with the family for decades. How much more trusted can you get?"

"What, did he just snap?" Scott asks.

"Naw," Reuben says. "I think he saw it as his last chance to get rich before he died."

Wood crackles in the bonfire. A big wave crashes against the shore. Small white clouds look like cotton against the blackness of the sky.

"I still don't get it," Scott says. "I mean, mimicking Di's accent is nowhere near as embarrassing as losing your lunch on the Homecoming Queen."

"That wasn't the embarrassing moment," Reuben says, looking down at his hands.

"That's the only one that comes close as far as I can tell," Scott says.

"Yeah, right now you kinda sound like a hero," Michael adds.

"Well, actually," Reuben says, "I left out the embarrassing part. When the flashlight went out the second time, I kissed Di."

"So what's wrong with that? I woulda done it," Benjamin says.

"Me, too."

"And me."

The rest of the group choruses their agreement. Reuben has not looked up from his hands. He clenches them into fists.

"And she said, in a very calm, mannered voice, 'Lester, I do believe one of your friends has just committed a crime against the state.'"

Someone chokes back a laugh.

"Shows she's got a sense of humor," Benjamin says at last.

"A vicious one," Reuben says. He turns his head away from the bonfire so that the group can't see his expression. "'You should tell him,' she continued, 'that the next time he plans to kiss a Princess, he should brush his teeth first.'"

"Jeez," someone says.

"And then she started laughing, only she wasn't making a sound, so I thought she was crying."

The group is silent, all imagining themselves at the side of the Princess of Wales who, although she is old, is hot. Then they all imagine she is so grossed out by their kiss that she says something about it. They shudder in unison.

Finally Scott, who feels responsible for prying this story out of Reuben says, "Hey, man, I bet no one knew it was you. All the waiters were Lester's friends."

Reuben shakes his head. "At that very moment, the lights came up. The only waiter who was blushing was me."

Silence again. Unlike the homecoming story which has, for these men, a slight undertone of an ice goddess getting her just desserts, Reuben's story carries its own level of pity. After all, the embarrassment is on an international scale.

"Then what?" Michael asks softly.

"What do you mean 'then what'?" Reuben says.

"What did you do then?"

Reuben licks his lips and glances at a faraway place none of them can see. "She took my hand and, wiping the tears from her eyes, said, 'If you are a love and bring me my tea, I'll give you a right proper kiss.'"

"And did you get her tea?" Scott asks.

For the first time since dark, Reuben grins. "After I brushed my teeth," he says.

He looks at the cars parked in a line against the side of the road. Almost as if on cue, a cellular phone inside one car rings for the sixth time in the last hour.

"Aren't you ever going to answer that?" Scott asks.

Reuben shakes his head. "She'll call back," he says. "She always does."

# Loop

$A$MELIA COULD NOT BELIEVE she was actually sitting there. The log was cold and damp beneath her jeans. The trees above dripped water. Out in the mist, an owl called, followed by the faint echo of a dog barking. Laughter from the porch made her cringe.

Above the ground fog, the sky was clear. Stars twinkled and a tiny satellite made its consistent way around the heavens. Her cheeks tingled with chill.

She could still feel the controls, clutched in her left palm. The sharp plastic edges bit into her skin.

Somehow she hadn't imagined it would be like this. Somehow she had thought the device would send her into the middle of an extended memory: *she* would be sitting on the porch, Tyler's hand warm on her knee, Jeanne and Paul beside them, the smell of eggnog in the air. She had wanted to relive it all, not observe it from the side.

"More eggnog anyone?" Tyler's voice had a deep richness. It warmed her. She longed to crawl onto the porch, knock her old self out of the way, and sit beside him again.

She had tried that when she first arrived. Her hands went through them all—and they hadn't noticed. She felt like Emily in *Our Town*: trapped in the best memory of her life, and no one saw her.

"Me," her own voice replied. It sounded higher, more confident than it did from the inside.

"Yeah, and a little more rum," Paul said.

"None for me." Jeannie's southern accent had an air of falseness. Amelia didn't remember her well. Paul had broken up with Jeanne after dating her for only a year.

A long time ago.

It had all been a long time ago.

Amelia got up off the log, brushed the water off her jeans (—how could she feel that and not her friends on the porch?—), and let herself in the back door. The kitchen was as she remembered it: done in browns and tans, filled with too many dishes, too many books and too many papers. The room smelled like turkey and pumpkin pies cooled on the counter. A calico cat—Nerdboy! She hadn't thought of Nerdboy in years—slept on an overstuffed kitchen chair.

Tyler stood over a large punchbowl filled with egg-nog batter. With his right hand, he poured a steaming bowl of hot rum into the mixture. His dark hair curled over his collar, and his broad shoulders strained at his denim workshirt.

She had forgotten how slim he was, how graceful his movements. As she walked toward him, Nerdboy looked up. His tail thumped against the chair, and his ears went back. He growled.

Tyler half-turned. "What is it, Nerdie?"

She froze there, waiting for him to see her. Nerdboy growled again.

"There's nothing there, kiddo," Tyler said, and returned to the eggnog. In the living room, the opening strains of the Elvis Presley version of "Blue Christmas" blared before someone turned the stereo down.

"Hey, you hiding in there or what?" Paul yelled.

"Coming!" Tyler ladled eggnog into three glass cups, looped his fingers through the handles, and carried them into the living room. Amelia followed. A fifteen foot Douglas fir dwarfed the room, decorated only in colored lights and clear glass balls. Elvis crooned in the background, and brightly wrapped packages huddled under the tree. Her younger self patted the couch for Tyler. He handed Paul a cup before sitting down.

Her younger self looked up and the smile froze on her face. She grabbed Tyler's wrist, nearly spilling some eggnog on his shirt. "Tyler, look. There she is again. That woman."

Tyler set his cup on the coffee table before looking up. Amelia didn't move. She wanted them to see her. She wanted *him* to see her. "Hon, it's shadows."

"No," Paul said. "I see someone too." He stepped out of the living room. Amelia walked toward him. If Paul believed, then Tyler would too. Then she could touch him again—

She squeezed the controls tightly, holding her breath as Paul walked into the darkened hallway. The machine squealed, and light shattered around her.

\*\*\*

SHE COULD SEE NOTHING for what felt like an eternity. Then the white light faded into red and green spots. The air was warm, warmer than it had been in the house. She didn't move, uncertain of where she was.

The spots cleared and she found herself in the lab. The lab was as empty as it had been when she got there hours—a day?—ago. The forlorn Christmas tree left a pile of needles on the tiled floor. The Happy Holidays banner had come loose from its nails and the middle sagged. Dirty cups sat on the worktables and gift-wrap overflowed from the wastebaskets.

It took a moment before she focused on the figure sitting in the middle of the mess. It was another version of herself—the version she had seen in the mirror that morning—fifty-six, slightly overweight, with deep, sad lines forming around her mouth, and silver hairs overpowering the black ones in her short haircut.

Something was wrong. She shouldn't be able to see herself. Not here. Not in the now. She should be *in* herself, experiencing the moment from the inside.

Perhaps that was a moment from her past. Perhaps that was what she had looked like before she had gone to the memory. Perhaps she hadn't come all the way back.

She looked down at the controls, but they were still hidden by that incredibly bright light. She couldn't feel her left hand.

Tyler would have known what to do. Tyler always test-ran the equipment, while she stayed back and monitored the progress from the Now-station. Only no one was monitoring for her. No one could see if the small red malfunction light was blinking.

*It would be so easy,* she had said to herself after having too much rum and eggnog alone in that big empty house. *Just a little trip back, set for only ten minutes: routine. No one would argue with routine.*

No one would even notice. No one was scheduled to return to the lab until the day after New Year's, and that was Mark and Christy, the junior team, who would test all the equipment to see if everything was running properly for the week's experiments. Mark and Christy were grad students who had only been on the Project since Tyler died. Even if they saw the malfunction button blinking, they wouldn't know what to do about it.

Not that it mattered. No one had survived in the time stream this long. Tyler had thought it impossible to last more than a day. The government forensic experts who had autopsied him had thought some temporal distortion had killed him. They had warned her to pick the next traveler carefully—someone young with a lot of stamina and no family history of severe medical problems. Having anyone else travel would jeopardize the government funding and the Defense Department approval.

Amelia didn't know how long she had been in the stream. Tyler had never mentioned a white light.

She closed her eyes and reached for her left hand. Her fingers encountered fabric. She followed it until she felt her left wrist bone—with her right hand, as if it were someone else's wrist—then slid her fingers around to the controls. The plastic was cold. She couldn't feel any of the indented keys. She fumbled, reached, and heard an explosion loud as a clap of thunder.

\*\*\*

THE SUN WARMED HER FACE. Her back was wet. An odd tingling ran up her left side. Her left arm had gone to sleep. She opened her eyes and found herself staring at a sky so blue it looked like it had been painted by a child who loved bright colors.

Water lapped around her, pushing at her clothes, raising her off the ground and then retreating. A hesitant lover, uncertain of his touch. She smiled and reached for Tyler as she had every morning since she was twenty-five.

He was gone.

She sat up, memory returning. Her left arm dragged in the sand, the control fused to her hand as if she too were made of some sort of synthetic. The sand was white, the air humid. The branches on the palm trees swayed with the gentle breeze. To her left the ocean stretched as far as she could see. To her right, the beach ended in a rise that led to a modified Spanish adobe.

Amelia had never been here before.

She stood. Her arm swung heavy and useless beside her. Water dripped off her hair, and down her clothes. Her tennis shoes were soaked. That sensation bothered her most of all. She slipped off one shoe, then the other, picked them up and walked barefoot across the hot sand.

Halfway to the adobe, her feet encountered stone. The stone path led through a hedge of oversized ferns. She walked through it and stood on a rise overlooking a shaded verandah. Small groups of white wicker furniture surrounded a small swimming pool. Two large glass doors were propped open. Thin white curtains blew inside the house, revealing more white furniture and a white carpet. A serving tray bearing a glass filled with brown liquid floated by itself through the double doors. It stopped near one of the furniture groupings.

"…can't." A woman's voice floated up toward Amelia. Amelia walked down the rise beside the pool, looking for the source of the voice.

A young woman sat in one of the wicker lounge chairs, slim legs crossed at the ankles. She wore a sheer white wrap with bikini bottoms underneath. Her feet were bare. Her right hand rested on a glass table, the beverage beside her. The serving unit floated back toward the house.

"I know this isn't the most festive place to spend Christmas. But—" her voice broke "—Grandmama's funeral is tomorrow, and all the relatives will already be here."

Amelia couldn't see the phone at all, but she knew it had to be there. The young woman was speaking into the air. Amelia wondered how the young woman heard the voice on the other end. She walked closer, remaining half-hidden, uncertain if the young woman could see her.

Then she stopped. The young woman had long black hair, a narrow face, and wide dark eyes.

She looked like Tyler.

She looked exactly like Tyler.

Amelia sat on one of the wicker chairs near the pool. Her left hand bumped the edge of the chair, sending a dull ache to her shoulder. The unit squealed and light eased out of its sides. The fingers on her right hand tingled.

A lump rose in her throat. She and Tyler had never had children. On purpose. So what had brought her here, to this woman, near Christmas? It was somewhere beyond Now, somewhere in the future, judging by the devices. Had Tyler had a child he hadn't told her about? He had had so many relationships before they met.

"No, look. I'm sorry," the young woman said. "I can't talk any more." She moved her right hand slightly and sighed. The connection had been severed somehow. Then she sat forward and squinted in Amelia's direction.

"Grandmama?"

The young woman reached for Amelia.

"Grandmama?" she repeated.

The light grew brighter. Amelia reached back. Their fingers met, but did not touch. Instead, the light engulfed her, and she could no longer see.

\*\*\*

THE GIFTS WERE OPEN. Brightly colored wrapping paper lay in shreds on the floor. Paul and Tyler sat cross-legged on the hardwood floor, playing with matchbox trucks. Jeanne and Amelia's younger self leaned on the back of the couch, arms crossed, and made snide comments about boys always being boys.

Amelia stood next to Paul. His red truck skid across the floor and went through her feet. Her entire left side tingled, and the tingle had grown in her right fingers. She wanted to kneel next to Tyler and ask him what was happening. She wanted him to reassure her that everything was all right.

But everything was not all right. She was wasting away. Tyler had had the same symptoms, spread over a longer period.

She crouched, her left hand scraping the smooth wood floor. Paul started, then slid back, grabbing Tyler's arm as he moved. "There she is," Paul said.

"Where?" Amelia's younger self stepped forward. Jeanne followed.

Tyler looked up. "I don't see anything."

"Jesus," Paul said. "It looks like your mother, Amelia."

"Mother was never in this house," Amelia's younger self said.

Amelia remained still. She met Paul's gaze steadily.

"Where?" Tyler asked.

"Right next to me," Paul said.

Suddenly Tyler saw her. She recognized the light in his eyes. "My God," he said. He got up and walked around her. She stifled the urge to move with him. Then he tried to put his hand on her shoulder. She leaned into the touch, but his hand went right through her.

"My God," he repeated. "This isn't your mother, Amelia. This is you."

Amelia nodded. Tyler jumped back.

"This isn't possible," Amelia's younger self said. "I'm right here. I'm alive."

"And so is she." Tyler crouched in front of Amelia. His cheeks were flushed. "You can hear me, can't you?"

"Yes," she said.

"Yes," he whispered. "But I can't hear you." He tried to touch her again, and frowned as his hand went through her. "It's some kind of distortion field. You're not a ghost at all."

"I'm alive," Amelia said. She had to repeat it twice before Tyler understood.

"It is a distortion field. Time experiments?"

The older Tyler would have yelled at her for giving his younger self that much information, but she didn't know what it would hurt now. He had already seen her.

She nodded.

"My God," he said. "They work."

She shook her head and touched her arm. "Help me," she said. "Please. Help me."

"She's asking for help," Paul said. "Tyler—"

But Paul's voice was fading. The light had returned: brighter this time. It burned into her left hand, along her side. She cried out in pain—and then the light engulfed her.

***

COLORS FLASHED BEHIND her closed eyelids. She was on a cold, hard floor. Her head ached. She sat up and rubbed her forehead with her good hand before opening her eyes.

The lab again. Her Now-self still huddled over the controls like they were her last link to sanity. She stared at her Now-self for a moment. Had she really looked that lost before stepping into the time stream? She used to pity women who looked like that after they had lost their man. Tyler had been dead six months. She still had the experiments, their house, their friends.

But they all felt so empty without him. An ache grew in her chest.

*It's a dream,* Tyler had said. *We're living a dream.*

She made herself get up. She swayed a bit, unused to moving without the help of her left arm. She walked around the benches to her Now-Self. Her Now-self was fiddling with the controls. Amelia remembered that moment: she only had time to return to one memory. She had to make it a good one.

Odd that she hadn't picked one with her and Tyler alone.

But she had been thinking Christmas, since it was the loneliness of the holidays that had driven her to the lab in the first place. And the best Christmas had been that first one in the country house, with Paul and Jeanne. She and Paul and Tyler had always compared the others to that one, thinking that nothing could measure up.

But it didn't really seem that special now. Perhaps it had been special because it had been the first.

Her Now-self looked up and gasped. Amelia sat on the bench across from her. Her Now-self reached out just as the air exploded around them.

\*\*\*

SHE COULDN'T GET AIR. Her mouth was filled with water. Her right arm flailed. She opened her eyes to a blue distorted world. Underwater. She was under water. She had to reach the surface or she would drown.

She kicked up, three good strong kicks that pushed her to the air. She spit the water out of her mouth and took deep, thankful breaths. Water rippled around her. Her presence had disturbed it. She was in a pool. The pool she had seen near the adobe house. She kicked her way to the ladder on the pool's deep end, and grabbed onto the metal railing with her right hand. The tingling had progressed into her wrist. She could barely move the hand at all.

She was running out of time.

She climbed out and sat on the side, breathing heavily. The young woman was asleep in her lounge chair, left arm covering her beautiful face. Amelia knew better than to try and touch her. The people were not real but the places were, as if they were a revolving set for a cosmic play.

Amelia grabbed a towel off the stack and wiped the water from her face. The humid air almost felt cool. She wrapped the towel around her neck, and wandered inside the house.

The main room was white with white furniture: obviously for entertaining. The back rooms had beds in them with clothes scattered about. The young woman did not live alone. A cat slept in the middle of one of the beds, and gave Amelia the evil eye as she passed.

She stopped in the only bedroom that looked as if it hadn't been used recently. The bed was an oversized four-poster like the one she and Tyler had had, with pale pink sheets under a pink and brown patterned spread. But that wasn't what drew her. What drew her were the pictures on the walls.

Some looked familiar: an early date with Tyler at a seafood place; a prize-winning photo of their first lab. But others were dream photos: her in a white wedding gown, Tyler in a black tux smiling down at her; both of them smiling in professional photography fashion at the tiny baby she held in her arms. Then baby pictures and school pictures of a young girl surrounded by family groupings with Tyler aging as he had and the temporal distortion wasting him away. He wore another tux for the young girl's wedding, looking proud and fatherly, and after that, he appeared in no more pictures even though they continued to chronicle the girl, and then her daughter—the young woman Amelia had seen outside.

She sighed and leaned on the bed. Her body was shaking. A life that she hadn't lived, complete with photographs. This had probably been her room until she died.

The shaking turned into a shudder. A life she hadn't lived. A life she could never live, even if she had married Tyler and had a child. She would die in this time stream—in this loop—and no one would know. They would just think she had disappeared.

She stared at the photos, and watched as they vanished in a blur of light.

***

SHE AWOKE TO THE SOUND OF VOICES. Tyler was hunched over her, a frown on his too-young face. "She's back," he said.

Amelia couldn't move either arm. She wanted to sit up, but knew she didn't dare, not in front of this young Tyler, not with the chance of losing her balance.

"What's happening to you?" he asked.

She wished he could hear her. She would tell him and maybe he would find a solution. Still, it wouldn't hurt to try. "I'm trapped," she said. "I'm stuck in a loop."

He understood the part about being trapped. She had to repeat herself three times before he said: "Loop? Like in the movies?"

Not exactly, because she did move forward in each time period. She just kept visiting the same three settings. But she nodded anyway.

"Loop," he said reflectively. The tree lights winked behind him.

"I still think she's a ghost," Paul said, from somewhere behind them. "I don't care about the scar on the chin. She looks like Amelia's mother."

Tyler shook his head just a little. He smiled at her with the love she had missed. He knew her, just as she would have known him. It didn't matter that she had a younger self watching somewhere in the background.

The light was back, eating Tyler, making him disappear. The loops were shorter now. "Tyler," she said, wishing she could reach for him. She didn't want to lose him again—

\*\*\*

—BUT WHEN SHE CAME TO HERSELF she was back in the lab, propped against the large black lab table near the front of the room. The numbness had started in her feet. She looked at her arms. They seemed to be hers, except for her left hand, with the control fused to her skin.

She had jumped back too far. She had known there would be that risk. Tyler had said that when he went on trips longer than ten years he always felt depleted. But she had thought she could deal with depleted.

Her Now-self left the bench and walked over to Amelia. Her Now-self wore a ring on the third finger of her left hand. Had Amelia altered something by appearing? Or had she slipped into another life, another time? Had that trapped her?

Her Now-self's hands were shaking. They passed over Amelia's useless left hand, and her Now-self swallowed, hard. "Your control is broken," her Now-self said.

"I know," Amelia said.

But her Now-self was looking down and didn't seem to hear. Even in this place, she couldn't speak to herself.

Her Now-self set the control down. "Here," she said. "If I don't touch it, you can. Take mine."

Amelia shook her head. She couldn't move her arms. She smiled a little sadly. She would die here.

"You're the woman we saw all those years ago, aren't we?" Her Now-self asked.

Amelia nodded. She was getting too tired to speak.

"You went to see him, didn't you?" Her Now-self asked. "Just like I was going to."

Amelia smiled a little. She *had* seen him, one last time. And he had smiled at her. He loved her, no matter who or when she was.

"And it was wrong. It trapped you." Her Now-self stood. "When he—when he was alive, he made me promise to never come here by myself. He knew, didn't he?"

"He guessed," Amelia said, even though her Now-self couldn't hear.

"And all the precautions," her Now-self said quietly. "He was trying to protect me. He said, before he died, that he would always love me. And I didn't believe him. I had to see—"

Amelia nodded. The tingle filled her entire body. The light was returning, and the sound was fading. She had done this. She had made the changes, by appearing in her own past. As a ghost.

She wanted to tell her Now-self not to go, but she couldn't. She couldn't move at all.

\*\*\*

THE LIGHT FADED ONE FINAL TIME. Amelia knew something supported her, but she couldn't feel it beneath the tingle in her body. As the red and green dots dissipated, she found herself on the four-poster bed in the adobe house, staring at the pictures on the wall.

They hadn't changed: she and Tyler gazing happily at each other, the baby between them; Tyler, giving away the bride. It took a moment before she understood what the photographs meant. They meant that her Now-self had heard, had understood. Her alternate self, the one who had married Tyler, born a child, and worked on the project, had set the controls aside, faced the dark and lonely house, and conquered it.

A breeze moved the curtains. The air had a fresh, salty smell here that she could have grown to love. A movement caught the corner of her eye. She tried to turn her head, but couldn't. The floorboards creaked, and the young woman in the white shift appeared at the edge of Amelia's vision.

"Grandmama," the woman said, kneeling beside the bed, "Grandmama, I miss you so."

Amelia smiled her last smile at the woman she and Tyler had helped make in a world she would never remember. "I missed you too, honey," she said as the light took her. "I missed you too."

# Boz

*B*OZ WOKE UP SLOWLY, convinced he was hearing an ancient crooner sing "White Christmas." He pulled his pillow over his head to drown out the noise before he remembered where he was.

Space. The ship. Light years from anything.

Christmas carols? He'd never expected to hallucinate them.

He sat up. His room was filling slowly with light. The on-board systems had been set up to mimic a typical Earth day (as if a typical Earth day had constant sunshine), and they did adjust for the seasons.

When the *Beautiful Dreamer* had been in the planning stages, the crew decided two things: that they'd remain on a 24-hour day, and they'd follow the western calendar. He didn't mind the 24-hour day, but he saw no reason to keep the calendar. He had voted against it and had been out ruled, which was funny, given that he was going to be the only one awake to "enjoy" that calendar.

He sighed, rolled over, and pulled the pillow off his head. Sure enough, some 20th century icon was singing about Christmas. Only the song had changed to "I'll Be Home for Christmas." That was a cruel joke. No one on this ship was going home again.

Not that Boz cared. He hadn't had a home in decades.

He sat up, rubbed his hand through his scraggly hair, and asked, "Computer, what's the date?"

The computer answered in its relentlessly cheerful voice, "December 25."

Christmas.

"I'll be go to hell," he whispered, and then shivered.

The music wasn't playing in the computer speakers. If it was, he would have heard it directly in his room. Instead, it sounded far away, as if someone were playing tunes down the hall.

(It actually sounded just like it used to when he lived alone in New York: Christmas music would waft at him from everywhere—his neighbor's apartment, the nearby storefronts, the street below. He shivered again, not liking that memory. Those days before he'd joined the mission had been difficult ones.)

"Make the music stop," he said.

"I do not register any music." When the damn thing was being negative, the voice grated all the more.

"Well, somebody's playing some, and there's just you and me on this ship." He slipped on clothes, something he promised himself he would do no matter what, because he *was* working, even if the circumstances were odd.

"Correction," the computer said. "There are 656 individuals on this ship. *I* am not an individual. I am a construct designed to…"

"I *know*." He wished he hadn't spoken aloud. He sighed and tried again. "Has someone awakened accidentally?"

"All of the sleep chambers are functioning properly. The crew is unchanged."

"Then where is the music coming from?" Boz asked.

"I do not register any music. Hearing things is a warning sign. Should I call up the holographic psychiatrist?"

"No," Boz said, and decided to stop talking to the computer. If the computer determined he was crazy, the damn thing would wake someone else up—with no hope of that person returning to cold sleep. Then Boz would be stuck with another person—a person who had been told he was ill, injured or had mental problems.

He couldn't cope with that.

The music had changed again. Now young people's voices rose in "Happy, Happy Holiday Time." At least that tune was a little more modern. The chorus of pure children's voices gave him a sudden longing for snow, of all things.

Snow and chill air and a breeze. What he wouldn't give for a breeze.

He stopped just inside his door, and leaned his head on the metal. He hadn't had this kind of homesickness since the first month. He'd been alone on this vessel for nearly a year, and for the most part, it hadn't bothered him, just like predicted.

He was an off-the-charts introvert, someone who would live alone even if he were given the choice to live with people he liked, someone who preferred his own company to everyone else's—at least, that was what all the battery of tests said. The tests had been strictly anonymous—done by number, so that the researchers wouldn't look at the subject's history. Once his number was revealed, all Boz's personal history did was confirm the diagnosis.

No marriages, no children, his parents long dead. Boz had lived alone since he was sixteen years old, and hadn't missed the company.

But the point wasn't ancient history. The point was Christmas carols—"Jingle Bells" now (what did that song mean, anyway?)—and the fact that the computer denied any knowledge of the sound.

Something had malfunctioned, oddly malfunctioned. He would find it.

He pulled open the door. The music got louder. He could hear piano and drums behind those children's voices, singing happily about dashing through snow (ooh, the longing *again*: he shook it off. He couldn't get lost in nostalgia—he had two more years of breezelessness ahead). The smell of hot cocoa warmed him, and made him think of the only Christmases he'd ever celebrated: those with his parents.

Hot cocoa?

He looked down. A tray sat just to the left of his door. A mug with something that looked like hot cocoa and steamed like hot cocoa sat on one edge of the tray. In the center, a coffee cake glistened, the frosting so fresh it slid off the side.

His stomach growled.

He bent down, and touched the tray. It was real. Had he ordered it? The three 'bots that had been brought along to make his life easier would put a tray out if he wanted it. He had never wanted one before.

He touched the mug, recognizing it as one of the ship's set. He only used his personal dishes, an affectation the captain called it, but part of the ritualized necessities that kept him going.

The shrinks had said that he wasn't mentally healthy—at least when it came to socializing—but he was exactly the kind of person to be left alone on the ship for the three years it took to get to the new colony. Initially, colony vessels like the *Dreamer* kept three or four people awake to handle back-up problems, but the monotony put them at each other's throats. More than one "accidental" death had changed that policy, and then the shrinks got involved.

Competent introverts were the answer.

Boz's problems faced him on the other end, when the ship reached the new planet's orbit, and he woke up the main crew. From then on, he would be in close contact with people, maybe for a year or more.

He worried about it, even now. He had actually told Captain McNeil that the required socializing disqualified him. Boz wouldn't be able to tolerate the living conditions, not just on the ship, but in the colony itself.

"We know," the captain said. Her pretty blue eyes twinkled. He'd often wondered how such a cheerful person had risen so far in the colony programs. "We have several solutions on the docket for you. You can study them as you travel."

His stomach clenched. He didn't want to think about the future. It scared him more than he wanted to admit.

Almost as much as the Christmas carols and the hot cocoa. He crouched, touched the mug, felt the warmth through the unbreakable synth ceramic. Then he stuck a finger in the liquid—very hot—and brought it to his lips.

Hot cocoa. He hadn't had that in years, hadn't thought to make it here either, even though the ship's stores had everything he could ever want.

Then he touched the coffee cake. It was warm too. He broke off a piece. It felt fresh baked.

He took a bite. It tasted like the pastries he used to get in New York, before he moved to Houston to begin training for the colony program. Rich, warm, delicately spiced. A taste of the past, one he hadn't even realized he missed.

The entire morning was unnerving him. Was this some kind of test? If so, who had derived it, and why do it now, when the ship was in flight? They couldn't turn back, and Captain McNeil had explained to him that they didn't want anyone else to wake up if at all possible.

He ate the coffee cake, sipped from the cocoa, but left it on the tray. Too much sweetness for him this early in the day. He pushed the tray aside—something to deal with later—and headed down the hall, toward the music.

Instrumental now. Something from the *Nutcracker Suite*. He'd never bothered to learn much about that thing—what he knew about most of the Christmas traditions, he'd picked up as part of the culture. In fact, he'd felt a little relieved to be away from the annual holiday-assault fest.

Christmas.

He hadn't even known.

The music grew louder as he reached the rec room. One of the bots stood outside, a tray of cookies on its head. Christmas cookies, with frosting and sprinkles, and happy holidays written in red and green across the tray itself.

"I didn't program you for this," Boz said to it.

"That is correct," it said in its mechanized little voice.

He let out a small sigh of relief. He had been starting to doubt his own memory.

"Then what's this all about?" he asked.

"You must enter the recreation room," it said.

"First, tell me what's going on," he said.

"You must enter the recreation room," it repeated. "Or have a cookie."

He flatted his palm against the door lock, then grabbed a cookie despite his best efforts not to, and stepped into the recreation room. The music was louder here. The entire place smelled like pine needles. He took a deep breath of the nearly forgotten odor.

In the corner, a tree leaned against the wall. The tree was decorated with tiny multicolored lights, and silver balls that reflected those lights. Beneath the tree, hundreds of presents glistened.

Garland hung around the room, and more lights hung from the ceiling. Their colors reflected on silver disks that lined the floor.

He took a step forward, and one of the disks shimmered. Then a hologram of Captain McNeil rose in front of him. The hologram was cheaply made—Boz could see through her to the tree—and winked in and out, as if it couldn't quite sustain the image.

"Merry Christmas, Boz," she said. The image paused. He sighed. It expected a response.

"Merry Christmas," he said.

She smiled. "I hope you don't mind the intrusion into your routine. We programmed this celebration before we left. We've used your file to design the best holiday we can for you."

The image paused again. He wasn't sure how to respond. Say thank you? For scaring him half to death? He couldn't say that. He couldn't say much of anything. He felt as tongue-tied as he would have if she were actually standing in front of him.

Finally, he managed, "Okay."

"We weren't sure about the music. We programmed our favorites. You can change that program now. The bots will prepare a roast turkey dinner for you with all the trimmings. You're welcome to have it whenever you like."

Her eyes twinkled, even in the damn hologram.

"But do open the presents. Each member of the colonizing team brought something they thought you'd appreciate, something you could watch or read or study in the long years ahead."

His mouth was dry. They gave him presents? Why?

"We wanted to tell you how much we appreciate you guarding our ship for the next few years," Captain Mc-Neil's hologram was saying. "We know you wouldn't be able to take the thanks personally, and thanks means so much less when the task is actually completed. So we thought we'd say it now."

The other disks sprang to life. All 656 colonists stood before him, most miniaturized so that they could fit into the room. He took a step backwards.

Six-hundred-and-fifty-six people staring him—or the image of them staring at him—made him want to flee.

"Thank you, Boz!" they said in unison. "Merry Christmas."

And then, mercifully, they all vanished.

Even the captain.

He swallowed against his dry throat. The music changed—a chorus of out-of-tune voices lustily sang, "We Wish You a Merry Christmas." He had a hunch he was listening to the crew.

The door swished open behind him, and one of the bots entered, a tray of beverages on its round head.

"Mulled cider," it said. "Or coffee or spiced tea…?"

No matter how hard it tried, it didn't sound like a waiter. Boz smiled, in spite of himself.

He took the mulled cider, then sat on one of the couches, his heart still beating rapidly. He reached over and touched the tree. His fingers passed through the branches. Another hologram, only a better one than the disks that scattered on the floor.

Then he reached for a present, expecting his fingers to pass through them. But the box was real. He picked it up. His name was scrawled on it in an unfamiliar hand. The tag said the gift was from someone named Betsy Wilson.

He didn't remember a Betsy Wilson. He felt vaguely embarrassed about that. He picked up the gift, opened it, found a dedicated reader—something with a permanent battery and a voice-over function. He would no longer have to use the computer for his late-night reading.

Thoughtful. Bought with him in mind.

He understood what was going on. This was part of the program to ease him into the colony, to prepare him for the future.

He should probably resent it. Perhaps he should act cynically and say there was no warmth behind this gift.

But there was. The colonists could have integrated him in a thousand ways—he'd read about half of those ways on the first part of the journey (and hoped he wouldn't have to do them). This—this was heartfelt.

He sat on the couch for a long time, clutching his reader, sipping his mulled cider, taking cookies from the tray on top of the bot's head.

Then he made a decision.

The captain was right: Thank-yous after the fact didn't mean as much. He called up the computer log, and had the computer record the room. He hoped the recording would get his face, the absolute awe he felt. Because he wasn't good with words, especially words others would eventually hear.

But even he could say thank you.

And he did.

# Disaster Relief
## A Winston and Ruby Story

WINSTON'S UNUSUAL SENSE OF CHARITY began late on Christmas night 2004. He and Ruby, his familiar, were watching television in the living room, Winston slouched on his couch, Ruby curled at his side. She had her tail wrapped around her small body, and her yellow eyes focused on the roaring fire.

They had exchanged a few gifts—he had made her a cat-sized box bed out of sandalwood, and she had given him half a dozen mice in various states of decay. He'd known what it had cost her to give them up—she'd probably been saving them for that proverbial rainy day—so he'd thanked her and placed them in a drawer to deal with later. He knew better than to give them back. He'd tried that with the dead rabbit on his birthday, and had hurt her feelings so badly that she hadn't talked with him for nearly a week.

He was surfing, looking for something, anything, *A Christmas Story*, the horrible live-action version of the

*Grinch*, when he saw the Breaking News icon at the bottom of CNN's crawl.

"Change it," Ruby muttered. "It's probably some new tape from Osama Bin Idiot out to ruin the holiday."

She'd been calling him that since the presidential election. She didn't understand why someone didn't wrap their front paws around his throat and kick out his stomach with their back paws. At least she hadn't offered to get a familiar friend to sway his magical companion toward the dark side of magic to take care of the problem, like she had after 9/11. Then she had claimed she was taking the human approach to the problem, but Winston could see she was as broken up by the coverage as he had been.

He should have changed the channel; he realized that later. The moment he saw the Breaking News icon, the holiday really and truly was over even before he heard the word "tsunami" and heard that tens of thousands of people were feared dead.

Ruby shuddered against him as the initial video footage sent through some unbroken internet connection showed a huge wall of water sweeping a beach, overcoming a pool, and slamming into a hotel. She buried her face in her paws and pretended to sleep, but after a few moments, she asked that he mute the volume.

He did, for both of their sakes.

And he resisted the urge to go to the window, to look at the ocean several yards below the stone wall of his tiny house, and to make sure that the waves he saw were small ones, familiar ones, the ones that always appeared this late in the season on a moonlit night.

Instead, he'd sent what little money he had to the Red Cross, mostly by the same internet that had given him the early pictures and ruined his Christmas. And when he and Ruby had gone to the shop on Monday the 27th, the first time they'd been there since the spending spree the tourists had indulged in on the 24th, she had insisted he stop the car at the beachside hotels, particularly the tall exclusive resort hotel that vaguely resembled the one demolished in Thailand. Ruby had wanted to get out of the car, to make sure the pool was still there, to look at the distance between the ocean's edge and the patio on the hotel's lower level, but Winston wouldn't let her.

He was as shaken by the images that came out of Southeast Asia as she was, only he didn't admit it verbally. He just stocked the cliffside house with cans of Fancy Feast and bags of Friskies. He bought enough bottled water to last four months, and he found all kinds of dehydrated food for campers and some Meals Ready to Eat from a military supply store on the web. That, and bandages, and first aid kits, and emergency flashlights, and candles, and blankets, and everything else he could think of.

Because, he realized after weeks of watching that footage, when the tsunami hit the Oregon Coast, Seavy Village would be as cut off as Banda Aceh. It took three weeks for rescue teams to reach some of the most remote villages. He figured any tsunami here would be triggered by an earthquake that would level Portland and maybe even Seattle; by the time people thought of Seavy Village and Newport and Tillamook and all the other coastal towns, the residents would be on their own for a very long time.

His house would survive even the biggest tsunami. The cliff face he was on was made of lava rock, and the house was way above the historic tsunami line. But his store wouldn't survive a tsunami, so he made Ruby practice the run that they'd have to make to the Church of St. Peter at the top of the hill. He'd instructed Ruby to jump on his shoulder, and he would use what little magic he had to glue her there, so that she wouldn't get trampled or hurt or swept away.

He found himself thinking of disaster and destruction much more than he wanted to. He would look at the ocean as an enemy, not as his beloved home, and then he would imagine trying to survive here with his very little magic, his beautiful familiar, and no rescue in sight.

By the time Hurricane Katrina formed in the south Atlantic, he had stopped watching television and listening to news on the radio. He huddled in his little shop, playing classical music on the Bose system he'd indulged in, and mixing spells in the back.

The spells were for his mail order business. He made a small fortune selling tiny spells—an aphrodisiac here, a love potion there (nothing powerful, just enough to send little waves of attraction), a protection spell or a spell that gave the user just a little bit of courage. He couldn't do much; he was never a great mage. But that didn't matter. Most people didn't want a lot of magic; they just wanted a bit of hope.

It wasn't until he went to the nearby grocery store for his favorite sandwich (turkey on rye with avocado for him; tuna on white with cheese for Ruby) that he realized Katrina had gone from another hurricane disaster to a nightmare on the scale of the tsunami.

He wasn't going to tell Ruby, but she knew. She could tell just from his face. She made him turn on the radio, and when they got home, she pushed the remote for CNN all by herself. When she didn't like that coverage, she went to MSNBC and FOX and the BBC, then back again, staring at the water as it pooled in that famous city as if it were coming for her.

One night during that awful week—he couldn't remember which one; they all seemed to blur—when he sat at his computer to give more money to the Red Cross (and some in Ruby's name to the Humane Society), Ruby jumped on his lap.

"What about Boyce?" she asked before Winston could punch the send button, completing his first transaction.

"Boyce?" Winston asked, feeling confused. Boyce Theriot was a colleague of his. They exchanged ingredients, shared recipes for some smaller spells, and occasionally helped each other with tough clients.

Boyce Theriot lived in New Orleans.

Winston couldn't believe he had forgotten that. He had relied on that fact so many times. Boyce had gotten him ingredients that no one else could, at least not in the states, because of New Orleans' voodoo culture.

"I'm sure he's all right," Winston said, not wanting to think about it.

Ruby put a paw on his hand, guiding it away from the mouse and that click that would send a few hundred dollars into the ether.

"Would we be?" she asked, nodding toward the screen. "If it happened here?"

"Ruby, I've explained this. We don't have levees, and we're not in a hurricane zone—"

"I'm not stupid," she said in that tone she used when she was completely serious. She knew that the Pacific coast had its horrible storms—every winter they seemed to suffer what the Atlantic would call a Category 1 Hurricane—and it was only a matter of time before something bigger hit. But the Pacific coast seemed geared for wind and heavy rain. It was the tsunami, the earthquake, the threat of total annihilation, like that which had happened in Southeast Asia, that worried him the most.

"I know," he said, and slid his hand away from her very tiny, but very insistent paw. "I didn't mean to say you were stupid. I—"

"If something happens here," she said, "like the tsunami or the earthquake or if one of the volcanoes blows, would we be all right?"

She hadn't asked him this before. She had watched him buy the extra food and the bandages, watched him stockpile the blankets and the kerosene stoves, and hadn't said a word.

He'd been relieved about that. He didn't want to lie to Ruby, not that he ever had.

He wasn't sure he could lie to her, and keep her as his familiar.

"I don't know," he said. And that was truthful. He didn't know. The other correct, truthful answer would have been *it depends.*

"You don't know why?" She climbed off his lap and sat on the small square of desk right in front of the keyboard, careful not to touch the computer in anyway. She was good about that, good about most things, really, except when she wanted his attention.

"Because," he said, "if we're here in the house, we should be okay, and I have a plan for the store. But if we're on the other side of town, or at the river crossing, which is below sea level, we might not make it home. We might not be all right at all."

"And," she said as if she were the one making the point all along, "your magic can't help us. You can't teleport like some. You can't fly. You can't—"

"I know what I can and cannot do, Ruby," he snapped. Then his face heated. He didn't like yelling at her. But her litany sounded too much like all of his instructors. They had finally decided that he was the most inept of all mages, the kind who had such a minor talent that they were barely better than the non-magical. His skills were tiny, his knowledge of the magical world just about as small. Part of the problem, his mentor Gerry Bellier had said, was that Winston didn't even understand magic on the larger scale. It didn't make sense to him, like calculus wouldn't make sense to a three-year-old.

Only a three-year-old could grow into the mental skills that would enable him to understand calculus. Bellier implied that Winston would never understand the larger magicks. And so far, he was right.

"Boyce is more talented than I am," Winston said.

"But he runs a shop," Ruby said.

"A lot of mages do," Winston said. "It's a front."

"It's not his front," Ruby said. "It's his life. He's told you that."

"He's in the French Quarter," Winston said. "It didn't flood. He'll be all right."

She turned, slammed a paw on the return key, and somehow did not complete his Red Cross transaction. Then she hit the mouse with her tail, and suddenly they were in one of his favorite programs, Google Earth, flying over the entire country.

"Zoom in," she said.

He didn't ask where. He knew what she wanted to show him. So he found New Orleans, and on the old satellite pictures, taken before the disaster, the town looked like it always had.

His heart constricted.

"Type in his address," she said.

He did, and the program showed him the street, at the far end of the French Quarter, not too far from downtown.

"Now type in Charity Hospital," she said.

He did, and then closed his eyes. Boyce's shop wasn't that far from Charity. In fact, it seemed closer to downtown than the French Quarter proper. Had Boyce lied on his website, just to attract more business? Or were there some peculiarities that Winston didn't know about New Orleans, about the way it counted its neighborhoods, about the way it labeled its subcultures?

"Seems to me," Ruby said, "that little shop of his is filled with water. Where does he live?"

Winston didn't know. He'd known Boyce for nearly thirty years, and yet they hadn't spent time together since they were young apprentices in San Francisco. He'd never seen Boyce's home and Boyce had never seen his.

They had become business acquaintances and nothing more.

"Maybe I don't understand all this human money stuff and everything," Ruby said, "but it seems to me if he earned a comparable income to yours in that city, he wouldn't be living in the Garden District. He'd be living somewhere that's also underwater. You think he's lying on his roof somewhere, waiting to be rescued?"

Winston winced. He didn't want to think about it. He wanted to go back to the previous screen and finish his donation to the Red Cross.

"Do you?"

"I could do a locate," Winston said feebly.

"And then what?" Ruby asked. "You can't just teleport him here."

"I know my weaknesses," Winston snapped. "Stop reminding me."

"Stop acting like someone with no magic at all. You have a friend here. Help him."

Winston stared at her. The sentiment was amazingly uncatlike. Cats did not help others in need.

Winston frowned. "Why do you care?"

She raised her chin. The whiskers on the end of it twitched, but the ones on her nose did not. The look she gave him was regal, and it implied that he was the stupid one in the room, not her.

"It could be us," she said. "We might be on our roof one day. We could be stranded here. I would hope someone would care enough to find us. I would hope that someone would care enough to help."

The thought was alien to him. He never expected help. He had had such a difficult childhood that when he became a mage, he didn't even expect help from a familiar. That had gotten him into trouble in his early years. An aphrodisiac he'd designed had gone bad because he hadn't had a familiar. His client nearly died, and he fled San Francisco with the police on his heels. They thought he was dealing drugs, and by his refusal to use a familiar, he probably had been. Magic made herbs special. Herbs without magic were simply cheap ways of getting high.

"You never thought of getting help, did you?" Ruby sighed.

"We're going to be on our own, Ruby," he said.

"Well, Boyce shouldn't be. No one should be. Jeez." She exhaled a mouthful of tuna breath so strong it almost knocked him over. Then she jumped on his thighs hard enough to give him bruises.

She left the computer and went back to her fireplace, sitting with her back to him, just to make sure he got the message.

What would he do if he located Boyce? Tell the authorities where to find him? They were already overburdened. He wasn't going to go to New Orleans. He wasn't the kind of man who went into a disaster zone, and for all her tough talk, Ruby wasn't the kind of cat who went there either.

She barely liked to leave the house, tolerating the ride to the shop only because she saw it as part of her turf as well.

Her anger radiated out toward him. He could feel it as if it were his own. Later, if he learned that Boyce had died and he could have done something to prevent the death, he would feel guilty. So guilty, in fact, that it might cripple him, just like that incident in San Francisco had.

"All right," he said. "We're going to do a locate. For whatever good that'll do."

Ruby's ears flattened but she didn't turn around. She didn't believe him.

He got up and went to the small closet where he kept his personal supplies. He got a few herbs, mixed a tiny potion, and dipped his fingers in it. Then he recited the spell in English, because his Latin was atrocious, and leaned back.

A puff of smoke appeared between him and Ruby. In it, he saw a high school cafeteria filled with hundreds of cots. Aid workers passed out cards or certificates or some kind of identification—he couldn't tell—to the left of the vision; to the right, a guard stood at the door, watching people as they went in and out.

Winston didn't see Boyce, not that he was sure he'd recognize him even if he were there. In the last thirty years, their only interaction had been on the phone. And, it seemed, everyone in that cafeteria had the same Southern accent—long, slow, and charmingly musical.

"I don't see him," Winston said, and the moment he spoke the words, a man sat up. He wore a raunchy t-shirt one size too small and a pair of blue jeans a size too big. His hair was thin and pulled back into a ponytail. But his eyes were the same. They were almost silver and they accented his café au lait skin, making him seem exotic and magical at the same time.

He looked through the smoke at Winston. Then he tilted his head. "Who don't you see?" he asked.

Ruby trotted to Winston's side. Winston leaned forward. "Boyce?"

"Winston? Winston Karpathian, is that really you?"

Everyone around Boyce was staring at him as if he'd gone crazy. It would seem that way too, if they had no magic. They wouldn't be able to see inside the smoke hole at the opening he had created in their corner of the universe.

"It's me," Winston said. "Where are you?"

"I dunno. Some podunk town that has more references to Jesus on its billboards than the churches in New Orleans do." He sounded lost.

"Hey buddy." The man next to Boyce touched his shoulder. "You all right?"

"Tell me the name," Winston said. "We'll get you out of there."

"Who're you? God?" Boyce asked. Winston had never heard such hopelessness in a man's voice before.

"Hell, no," said the man next to him, obviously thinking Boyce was talking to him. "I'm just trying to help."

"I can wire you some money," Winston said. "Call me, and we'll figure it out."

"Call you. You have a phone number?"

"What the hell?" the man next to Boyce stood up, vaguely offended. "Lemme get some help here."

Winston felt his own cheeks heat. Of course Boyce wouldn't have his phone number. That was in Boyce's shop, probably like everything else.

"Yeah," Winston said. He recited the number and added, "You can call collect."

Then the smoke ring faded. Ruby leaned against Winston, her little body tense. "That's a human shelter, huh?"

Winston nodded. A lot of the details hadn't registered for him until now: How many people had just curled up on their cots, staring at nothing; How no one really talked, except the aid workers; How the kids played listlessly in the corner.

He shuddered, and Ruby leaned harder, as if he could make things better.

And then his phone rang.

\*\*\*

THE NEXT FEW DAYS BECAME A BLUR. The $200 he was going to send to the Red Cross, and the $50 he was going to send to the Humane Society (which Ruby protested—she felt he should still send that money) went to a plane ticket that got Boyce Theriot out of northern Louisiana and to Portland, Oregon. Winston had to charge another $50 on his credit card—the one he kept for emergencies—to get one of those airport limos to pick Boyce up, because Winston couldn't do it.

His only car was a Gremlin, bought because he liked the magical name, and he'd had it almost as long as he lived in Oregon. He found the problem that made it belch blue smoke, but he knew the undercarriage was so rusted that one day it would simply fall off.

While he waited for the limo to show up, he cleaned the guest room. He hadn't had a guest since he moved into the cliff house decades ago, and the bed had gotten buried beneath books and blankets and trinkets he'd found. The job was larger than he expected, and he even had to use a cleaning spell—something he hadn't done in a decade—to get the dust out of the mattress. He went to the Factory Outlet store and bought fresh sheets, a new comforter, and towels. Ruby wanted to keep the new stuff for them, and let Boyce use the older things from Winston's bed, but that felt wrong to him.

Now that he had resigned himself to company, he wanted to do a good turn by him.

The limo arrived late Friday night. Winston watched through the front window as people piled out. In the glow of the streetlights against the dark sky, it almost looked like an art film version of those clown cars he'd seen as a child. More and more people got out until he thought the entire vehicle would collapse from their loss.

Ruby sat on the back of the couch, looking more like a cat than a familiar. She watched from a position that guaranteed she could see the people, but they couldn't see her. And she could run for the bedroom at a moment's notice.

Winston left her inside. He went onto his front stoop, watching as the tallest, thinnest of the group took a receipt from the limo driver. The air smelled clean and sharp; the wind was strong off the ocean, usually something he loved.

But he felt nervous now, as if he had plunged into a world he hadn't quite expected.

The limo drove off, leaving five people in the street. Only five. It had seemed like so many more.

"Winston?" The tall, thin man came toward him and he realized it was Boyce. He hadn't remembered Boyce being tall or thin, but now that he saw Boyce walk, he knew that this was his old friend. How could anyone forget that walk, which was half sashay, half swagger?

Winston stepped off the porch and plastered a smile on his face. He hoped he wasn't shaking. "Boyce," he said, extending his hand.

"I hope y'all don't mind, but I gathered a few more of us. When I realized we could do a locate, I did, and then they did, and well, we can be our own little magical shelter, right?"

*Our own little magical shelter* was, at the moment, Winston's home. But he didn't say anything. He couldn't turn these people away. He knew they had less than he had.

"There's not a lot of room," he said. "But we'll make do."

Then he realized that everyone—except Boyce—was carrying an animal. Of course. Familiars. He felt his heart sink just a little. How would Ruby react to a French poodle, two other cats, and a Chihuahua?

He wanted to warn her (in fact, he wanted to remind her that Chihuahuas weren't food) but he couldn't. He just hoped she figured this out. He opened his front door, and let the crowd inside.

They squeezed in. In addition to himself and Boyce, there were two more men and two women. Everyone looked a little lost. They all wore mismatched clothing, and their hair seemed in need of a comb. The animals clung to their mages.

Ruby still sat on the back of the couch, her yellow eyes wide. She looked at Winston as if demanding an explanation.

"I only have one extra bedroom," he said, "but it has a king bed."

As if that made a difference. As if five people could fit comfortably on that bed.

"If y'all don't mind, we can just pile up some blankets in the front room," one of the women said.

"Nonsense, Nurleen," one of the men said. "You women can have the bedroom and we men can stay out front."

Winston swallowed hard. He hated crowds. He didn't much like people, and he suddenly felt trapped here, in his own home. "We'll settle rooms in a minute," he said. "Let's do introductions first."

Introductions. He started by going over to Ruby and putting a hand on her back. She jumped. Then she crawled into his arms, just like the other familiars were doing. She watched as the introductions went around.

Nurleen Bremmer of Gulfport, Mississippi. She was heavyset and dark-haired, wearing a Metallica t-shirt and sweatpants that looked like they'd seen better days. Her home disintegrated around her and she was lucky enough to grab Princess, her white and gold cat (and familiar) before everything vanished in a haze of wind, rain, and water.

Wendi Phillips of Biloxi, Mississippi. She had red hair so bright it would've made Lucille Ball proud, and her French poodle looked dyed to match. Wendi wore her own clothes—she managed to fit some outfits and underwear in her purse, she later informed everyone—but that was all she had.

Palmer Kent of New Orleans stood beside Boyce, and looked smaller for it. Kent wasn't much bigger than a child, and the Chihuahua he had with him—named after the Rock—didn't help much.

And Savion DeChutney, from Moss Point, Mississippi, who didn't say much because he looked like he might burst into tears at any moment. He was dark, with ritual scarring that made him seem scary, but his cat—Noel—spoke for him half the time because he was so honored to be taken in by someone who understood him.

Then Boyce sighed. "Y'all know me. To stop you from asking, the hurricane got Riddell. One of my bookshelves fell over as the house started to go, and he was crushed…"

Boyce didn't finish. Riddell was both his dog and his familiar. One of those small little decorative dogs—since Winston had never met him, he hadn't paid much attention to the breed—but he knew the dog probably hadn't been much bigger than Ruby.

Ruby shuddered and looked at Winston's bookshelves as if they were the enemy. Maybe they were. All he knew was that he would have to comfort her later.

"We sure are honored, Winston, that you took the time and trouble to give up your home like this," Boyce said. "To be among like-minded people, I can't tell you…."

Winston smiled at them, unsure what to do next. He hadn't planned to give up his home, just to provide a haven. "I've got some stew on the stove," he said, thankful that he'd planned a large meal instead of something for two. "Let's eat and get to know each other."

\*\*\*

THE STORIES MADE HIM SAD. Wendi had a beauty shop in Biloxi—not the hairdressing kind, but the kind that with a bit of magic dust and a lot of pep made people feel like they had some worth. The shop was gone now. Nurleen taught sleight-of-hand to tourists, then did a full fledged David Copperfield-like show in one of the casinos. From there, she used a bit of magic to see someone who was sad in the audience, someone she could help with a touch or a small wish. Nothing big, just enough to keep her hand in the practice.

Savion was a supplier—that was how Boyce knew him—specializing in difficult-to-find ingredients for hard-to-make spells. His warehouse had collapsed in the wind when the hurricane had come aground, the items scattered.

"No insurance," he'd said, head down, dipping the french bread Winston had baked in his soup. "I mean, how do you tell adjusters that eye of newt actually has a value?"

And Boyce, who hadn't gone to his shop after the loss of his familiar. He couldn't face it—partly because he knew that part of New Orleans was under water. Instead, he used what little magic he could to get himself out of the city, and then, drained and spent and worried about casting spells without his familiar, he hitched a ride to the nearest shelter, which took him to the high school where Winston had caught up with him.

Everyone was tired, and sad, and lost, but grateful. Grateful to have a place to go, grateful to have something else to think about. The animals were quiet. They all eyed Ruby, knowing this was her turf, and she glared back at them, establishing herself as dominant.

But Winston wasn't sure how long that would last. She pretended to be tough, but she was soft at heart. He could feel her trembling as she sat on his lap, watching their guests.

When he finally took her into his bedroom that night—he wasn't willing to give up this little bit of personal space—she climbed onto the bed and closed her eyes.

"I'm sorry," she said. "I didn't know it would be like this."

She was so stressed she wasn't flirting with him. She wasn't acting tough. She seemed exhausted.

He lay down beside her and she crawled on his chest. She didn't purr.

"They can't stay," she said. "There's too much conflicting magic. I can't keep track of it."

"I know." He could feel it too, and that seemed odd to him. Usually he couldn't feel much magic at all.

She put her head on her paws, and stared at him. "What are we going to do?"

He sighed. He had saved some money. It was his emergency fund—enough for surgery if Ruby got ill or a repair to his house that he couldn't handle magically. He'd been trying to save for a new car, but he'd had trouble with that. The disasters across the country had tapped him— he gave money away instead of putting it in the bank.

He hadn't thought of the downside of his charity. He preferred to keep it like everything else in his life—

at arms length. But now there were five people in his house, four of whom he'd never met before, and one he hadn't seen in thirty years.

Five people, and he could barely stand having two people in his store at the same time.

He shuddered.

"Big boy?" Ruby whispered. "What're we gonna do?"

"I guess," he said, "we need to find a house."

\*\*\*

HOUSES WEREN'T HARD TO FIND in Seavy Village. It was a coastal resort town, filled with second homes, which the locals called weekenders. Most of those places were empty and half of them were for sale. Many that weren't were designated as vacation rentals.

It didn't take Winston long to find one big enough for the group. When he told the real estate agent who handled the rentals what it was for, she perked up.

"I'm sure we can get you a break on the rent," she said. "Maybe even get some local charity groups to kick in. You want me to check?"

He hadn't expected help from anyone else, seeing this as entirely his problem which he brought on himself in a moment of selflessness. He mumbled something like that, and the agent grinned.

"We all been hoping we can help the evacuees. Most of them just didn't come to Oregon or the coast. Everyone's been wanting to do something, though. Those images from the Gulf…" She shuddered. "It could just as easily be here, you know. We get bad storms and tidal surges and—"

"I know," he said, waving a hand. Her conversation was too close to the ones he'd had with Ruby. He didn't want to think about what-ifs. Thinking about what-ifs had brought him here, doing his good deed.

"Well," the real estate agent said with a smile. "Let me just see what I can do. No way should you handle this on your own."

And she stepped in. He felt relief which also made him feel guilty. Finally, a competent person handling the problem. Someone other than him.

By the end of the day, he had a fully furnished vacation rental with six bedrooms and three bathrooms, along with some donated clothes, food for the animals, and some cash for the evacuees. The reporter from the paper came to photograph them moving in, and asked for everyone's story. All of the mages looked confused when asked, and finally, the real estate agent had said that maybe the interviews should be done at a less traumatic time.

Still, the story ran the next day—*Gulf Coast Evacuees Find Home In Seavy Village*—and pictures of the mages, their "pets" and their meager belongings graced every single newspaper box in town.

Police Officer Scott Park, the only non-magical person who knew what Winston really did for a living, stopped into the store that afternoon. Winston was hiding in the back, hoping to have a little privacy. He'd hated the sound of the bell, worried that he'd have to be charming to a new customer, and was relieved to see that Park had come alone.

"Quite the good deed you did," Park said. Ruby was rubbing her head against his hand. He'd helped save her life once, but she'd adored him even before that. She had been the one—by talking with him—to convince him that magic was real.

"Didn't mean to have it publicized," Winston said.

Park shrugged. "They say there's no such thing as bad publicity."

Winston nodded, but couldn't meet Park's eyes.

"They're all friends of yours?"

"No," Winston said. "Just Boyce. He helped you and me with a case once, remember?"

"Yeah," Park said. "How come they can't just conjure repairs?"

The question made Winston bristle, even though Park hadn't meant to be rude. Winston ran a hand over the glass case that separated him from the rest of the store.

"I guess I'm not the only one with small magic," he said.

"You'd think that people with larger magic would make it all go away," Park said.

Winston raised his head. He hadn't thought of that. If he had the ability, he would have done it. He wondered if there was something in the magical rules that prevented it, something about calling attention to one's self.

But he couldn't think of anything. Helping a neighbor or a friend with a serious problem was usually considered white magic (depending on the spell), and white magic was fine.

"Guess not everyone's as good-hearted as you," Park said, scratching Ruby at the base of her tail. She was purring so loud that she could probably be heard on the street.

"I'm not good-hearted," Winston said.

Park grinned. "That's a matter of opinion, my friend."

Maybe it was. But a good-hearted man didn't force the people he'd invited into his home to move out the very next day. A good-hearted man didn't feel relief when the people he helped closed the door behind them. A good-hearted man didn't secretly hope he'd never see them again.

\*\*\*

BUT OF COURSE HE DID. He was their contact in Seavy Village, and they came to him with questions. He was surprised at how much he knew.

When Nurleen asked who to contact at the local casino about performing her magical act, Winston told her. When Savion remembered that he had had a supplier in Portland who might need his services, Winston had the phone number. When Wendi wanted to know the name of a spa that might like a hairdresser who knew how to make her clients feel special, Winston knew the best place to go.

Winston even knew of a magic store for sale farther up the coast that seemed to suit Palmer Kent just fine.

The owner wanted to get out of the area, and would take small payments, so long as they were guaranteed.

Winston didn't guarantee them—he didn't want that kind of financial burden—but Scott Park knew a banker who could (and did) arrange it all.

By the end of the first week, the group had a place to live, and four of them had work. Savion was heading to Portland in a few days, and Palmer was moving north. The women were so busy they barely spent time in the house.

That only left Boyce.

Boyce, who seemed lost without his familiar, Riddell.

Boyce, who had decided to spend his afternoons helping Winston in the shop.

\*\*\*

WINSTON COULDN'T SAY NO, even though he wanted to. He couldn't tell Boyce to leave him alone. Boyce had lost everything: his home, his business and, until he got a new familiar, his magic.

On his third day in the store, Boyce decided that Winston needed to redecorate.

Winston had kept the store the same since he opened it, decades ago. The front was filled with touristy impulse buys—toys, fake magic tricks, pinwheels. He had a few real antiques in the window, mostly bottles that looked like I-Dream-of-Jeannie bottles, and some harmless potions to one side.

The back, where he did most of his work, was blocked by a beaded curtain. In between the back and the front, he had a glass cabinet with his cash register on top, and some valuable stones inside.

Boyce had walked around the place, studying it as if he would get quizzed on it. When he noticed Winston watching, he said,

"Y'all need some color over on the north wall. And some carpeting starting just past the door there, with maybe a raised up area for people to sit. A red curtain might be nice instead of those beads. And some new product. I mean, really, what do tourists need with antique bottles? I ask you."

Winston hadn't answered. He'd let Boyce talk and draw up plans.

Ruby exhausted herself following Boyce everywhere, watching him make little drawings, glaring as he rearranged the existing merchandise. Her tail twitched every time she looked at him, and after a few days of this, her ears flattened too. She slept hard every night because she couldn't nap; she was too afraid he might actually start implementing his plans.

Winston knew Boyce didn't have the money to make the changes, and Winston wasn't about to loan him any. Winston liked his store the way it was. When Boyce finally left, Winston would put the merchandise back where it came from. But Winston didn't know when Boyce would leave.

They weren't talking about it. Boyce wasn't even searching for a new familiar.

Boyce did wait on the customers for him. Winston had a few local customers now that the newspaper articles had run. People were charmed to meet Boyce, and they bought small things to justify their presence in the store.

Winston mostly remained in the back, wishing he had Boyce's skill with people. Customers laughed and joked, told stories and exchanged information. No one had ever seemed so relaxed in Winston's place before.

He hated it.

He hated it all.

And he felt mean, petty and small for each little resentment. Boyce had lost his life, and now Winston felt like he was losing everything he valued in his, one tiny bit at a time.

That thought made him feel even smaller, and he tried to banish it. But it grew, like a blackness across his vision. He was growing afraid to mix new spells, afraid his resentment would color the magic.

Finally Ruby brought him a section of the local paper that someone had left near the front door.

She tapped an ad at the very edge of the back page.

*Seavy Village Eighteenth Annual Dog Show*
*Contestants from all over the country compete for these prizes...*

Winston frowned at it. "You're not a dog."

She rolled her eyes.

"You don't even like them."

"For Boyce," she whispered.

"You don't get familiars at dog shows," Winston said. "They're for showing off dogs that are already owned."

If Ruby could have put her paws on her hips like an angry woman, she would have. Instead, she settled for her glare and a quick twitch of the tail.

"I know how to find familiars," she said. "He needs to go."

So Winston contacted the convention center and signed up as a vendor. He made a few dog treats, some calming potions, and charmed a few collars. Then he sent Boyce to man the table, and hoped that would be enough.

*\*\*\**

BOYCE DIDN'T COME BACK for two days, and when he did, he had a hollow ragged look around the eyes.

"Did you know?" he asked as he came through the shop's door, carrying a box filled with the remaining merchandise, "how many animals got abandoned in the storms?"

Winston did know because Ruby followed the statistics. She wanted some kind of guarantee that she wouldn't get lost if a tsunami hit the coast. He continually promised her he'd do his best, but they both knew that might not be enough.

"They've got shelters in California taking some of the overload," Boyce said as he put the cash and credit card slips on the counter. He'd sold almost everything he brought. "They were doing a fundraiser at the show."

Winston stared at the money. Boyce had earned more in one appearance than Winston had earned all fall.

"Would you think it rude of me to volunteer down there? I know you got me this lovely home and all, but I'm rootless, Winston. And Miss Ruby here doesn't like me. I never did get on with cats."

"Pfff," Ruby said from a corner of the counter. "Like that's the problem."

Boyce glanced at her, started to say something, and then stopped. "I was just thinking that I could be useful, and much as I like helping you, you don't really need me. We both know that."

Winston swallowed. He didn't want to nod, didn't want to insult Boyce.

"I can hitch a ride with one of the volunteers. I have a bit of that money your locals gave me. The girls'd keep the house, if you don't mind a little friendly competition—"

Winston didn't see the women as any kind of competition at all. They were in different parts of the business.

"—and maybe I'd come back," Boyce said.

"You're not obligated," Winston said. "I just wanted to help."

Boyce grinned at him, then took his hands. "I know. And you have. You have no idea how much."

\*\*\*

NOT A LOT. That was how Winston summed it up later. He hadn't helped much at all. He had given the five a destination, true enough, but he hadn't sacrificed more than a few days of his time and a few hundred dollars of his money. In the end, most everything they'd received had come from the town, not from him.

And what bothered him the most was how much he had resented it. How much he wished for them to leave, for his quiet life to return.

Now that it was back, he felt only relief. And guilt for enjoying the silence. He'd tried to do something outside his nature. Somehow he had thought it would make him feel better. Instead, it left him feeling shaken.

He took some of Boyce's advice. He put a light blue paint on the north wall, and took on consignment some paintings of wizards and fantasy dragons from a local artist. He took some of the scarves he'd brought with him from San Francisco thirty years ago, and draped them on the shelves, adding even more color.

He didn't change the beads though, nor did he add a rug, which he thought would be a disaster in this wet climate. And he didn't add a sitting area. He didn't want the customers to stay any longer than they had to.

Ruby hated all the changes, until she realized that they brought in more customers, and more customers meant more pets for her. She preened at them, acted like a cat, and got a lot of attention. She even got her own write-up in the local paper as the most popular store cat in Seavy Village.

Her newfound fame didn't alleviate her fears, but Winston realized nothing would. Just like nothing would change the odd feelings he'd had since the first of the year.

Finally, at Christmas, he realized he was living each day as if a disaster was about to happen, worrying that he had done things wrong when he'd only done what he could. Instead, he needed to look at each day as a blessing, each moment he had with Ruby in his quiet house in his quiet town as a gift—one that could vanish at any moment, yes, but one that he needed to value just the same.

On December 26th, a year after the tsunami that started his strange journey, he got a phone call. Boyce was back in New Orleans, helping clean up the city.

He had a new familiar, a puppy born to one of the rescue dogs who'd made it to California.

"She's green," he said, "but she's enthusiastic. And she's polite. Kinda reminds me of Ruby."

Winston had almost laughed out loud at that. Ruby was never polite. And then he remembered: She had been polite in those days after the storm. She had been polite and considerate and frightened, just like he had been.

He congratulated Boyce, told his friend he admired his courage, and wished him the best. Then he hung up the phone and found his own familiar, huddled next to the fireplace.

She had stopped watching the television sometime in October, and he was grateful. Instead, she watched the flames. He picked her up, and held her close, feeling her little heart beat against his.

"It's okay," he said softly. "We're safe."

"For now," she whispered.

"For now," he agreed. Then he smiled at her.

"You got small dreams, Big Boy," she said.

He nodded. He liked his small dreams. And his small house. And his small life.

He liked it all, and he would enjoy it as much as he could, for as long as he could.

Ruby sighed and snuggled into his arms. He sank down onto the rug in front of the fireplace, and watched the flames, relishing the moment.

Moments—that was all they had. But, he was beginning to realize, moments were more than enough.

# Millennium Babies

TWO WEEKS INTO THE SECOND SEMESTER, she got the message. It had been sent to her house system, and was coded to her real name, Brooke Delacroix, not Brooke Cross, the name she had used since she was 18. At first she didn't want to open it, thinking it might be another legal conundrum from her mother, so she let the house monitor in the kitchen blink while she prepared dinner.

She made a hearty dinner, and poured herself a glass of rosé before settling down in front of the living room fireplace. The fireplace was the reason she bought this house. She had fallen in love with the idea that she could sit on cold winter nights under a pile of blankets, a real fire burning nearby, and read the ancient paperbacks she found in Madison's antique stores. She read a lot of current work on her e-book, especially research for the classes she taught at the university, but she loved to read novels in their paper form, careful not to tear the brittle pages, feeling the weight of bound paper in her hands.

She had added bookshelves to the house's dining room for her paper novels, and she had made a few other improvements as well. But she tried to keep the house's character. It was a hundred-and-fifty years old, built when this part of Wisconsin had been nothing but family farms. The farmland was gone now, divided into five acre plots, but the privacy remained. She loved being out here, in the country, more than anything else. Even though the university provided her job, the house was her world.

The novel she held was a thin volume, and a favorite—*The Great Gatsby* by F. Scott Fitzgerald—but on this night, the book didn't hold her interest. Finally she gave up. If she didn't hear the damn message, she would be haunted by her mother all night.

Brooke left the glass of wine and the book on the end table, her blankets curled at the edge of the couch and made her way back to the kitchen. She could have had House play an audio-only version of the message in the living room, but she wanted to see her mother's face, to know how serious it was this time.

The monitor was on the west wall beside the microwave. The previous owners—a charming elderly couple—had kept a small television in that spot. On nights like this, Brooke thought the monitor was no improvement.

She stood in front of it, arms crossed, sighed, and said, "House, play message."

The blinking icon disappeared from the screen. A digital voice she did not recognize said, "This message is keyed for Brooke Delacroix only. It will not be played without certification that no one else is in the room."

She stood. If this was from her mother, her tactics had changed. This sounded official. Brooke made sure she was visible to the built-in camera.

"I'm Brooke," she said, "and I'm alone."

"You're willing to certify this?" the strange voice asked her.

"Yes," she said.

"Stand-by for message."

The screen turned black. She rubbed her hands together. Goose bumps were crawling across her skin. Who would send her an official message?

"This is coded for Brooke Delacroix," a new digital voice said. "Personal identification number…"

As the voice rattled off the number, she clenched her fist. Maybe something had happened to her mother. Brooke was, after all, the only next of kin.

"This is Brooke Delacroix," she said. "How many more security protocols do we have here?"

"Five," House said.

She felt her shoulders relax as she heard the familiar voice.

"Go around them. I don't have the time."

"All right," House said. "Stand-by."

She was standing by. Now she wished she had brought her glass of wine into the kitchen. For the first time, she felt as if she needed it.

"Ms. Delacroix?" A male voice spoke, and as it did, the monitor filled with an image. A middle-aged man with dark hair and dark eyes stared at a point just beyond her. He had the look of an intellectual, an aesthetic, someone who spent too much time in artificial light. He also looked vaguely familiar. "Forgive my rudeness. I know you go by Cross now, but I wanted to make certain that you are the woman I'm searching for. I'm looking for Brook Delacroix, born 12:05 a.m., January first in the year 2000 in Detroit, Michigan."

Another safety protocol. What was this?

"That's me," Brooke said.

The screen blinked slightly, apparently as her answer was fed into some sort of program. He must have recorded various messages for various answers. She knew she wasn't speaking to him live.

"We are actually colleagues, Ms. Cross. I'm Eldon Franke…"

Of course. That was why he looked familiar. The Human Potential Guru who had gotten all the press. He was a legitimate scientist whose most recent tome became a pop culture bestseller. Franke rehashed the nature versus nurture arguments in personality development, mixed in some sociology and some well documented advice for improving the lot nature/nurture gave people, and somehow the book hit.

She had read it, and had been impressed with the interdisciplinary methods he had used—and the credit he had given to his colleagues.

"…have a new grant, quite a large one actually, which startled even me. With that and the proceeds from the last book, I'm able to undertake the kind of study I've always wanted to do."

She kept her hands folded and watched him. His eyes were bright, intense. She remembered seeing him at faculty parties, but she had never spoken to him. She didn't speak to many people voluntarily, especially during social occasions. She had learned, from her earliest days, the value of keeping to herself.

"I will be bringing in subjects from around the country," he was saying. "I had hoped to go around the world, but that makes this study too large even for me. As it is, I'll be working with over three hundred subjects from all over the United States. I didn't expect to find one in my own back yard."

A subject. She felt her breath catch in her throat. She had thought he was approaching her as an equal.

"I know from published reports that you dislike talking about your status as a Millennium Baby, but—"

"Off," she said to House. Franke's image froze on the screen.

"I'm sorry," House said. "This message is designed to be played in its entirety."

"So go around it," she said, "and shut the damn thing off."

"The message program is too sophisticated for my systems," House said.

Brooke cursed. The son of a bitch knew she'd try to shut him down. "How long is it?"

"You have heard a third of the message."

Brooke sighed. "All right. Continue."

The image became mobile again. "—I hope you hear me out. My work, as you may or may not know, is with human potential. I plan to build on my earlier research, but I lacked the right kind of study group. Many scientists of all strips have studied generations, and assumed that because people were born in the same year, they had the same hopes, aspirations, and dreams. I do not believe that is so. The human creature is too diverse—"

"Get to the point," Brooke said, sitting on a wooden kitchen chair.

"—so in my quest for the right group, I stumbled on thirty-year-old articles about Millennium Babies, and I realized that the subset of your generation, born on January 1 of the year 2000, actually have similar beginnings."

"No, we don't," Brooke said.

"Thus you give me a chance to focus this study. I will use the raw data to continue my overall work, but this study will focus on what it is that makes human beings succeed or fail—"

"Screw you," Brooke said and walked out of the kitchen. Behind her, Franke's voice stopped.

"Do you want me to transfer audio to the living room?" House asked.

"No," Brooke said. "Let him ramble on. I'm done listening."

The fire crackled in the fireplace, her wine had warmed to room temperature, bringing out a different bouquet, and her blankets looked comfortable. She sank into them. Franke's voice droned on in the kitchen, and she ordered House to play Bach to cover him.

But her favorite Brandenburg Concerto couldn't wipe Franke's voice from her mind. Studying Millennium Babies. Brooke closed her eyes. She wondered what her mother would think of that.

\*\*\*

THREE DAYS LATER, BROOKE was in her office, trying to assemble her lecture for her new survey class. This one was on the two world wars. The University of Wisconsin still believed that a teacher should stand in front of students, even for the large lecture courses, instead of delivering canned lectures that could be downloaded. Most professors saw surveys as too much wasted work, but she actually enjoyed it. She liked standing before a large room delivering a lecture.

But now she was getting past the introductory remarks and into the areas she wasn't that familiar with. She didn't believe in regurgitating the textbooks, so she was boning up on World War I. She had forgotten that its causes were so complex; its results so far reaching, especially in Europe. Sometimes she just found herself reading, lost in the past.

Her office was small and narrow, with barely enough room for her desk. Because she was new, she was assigned to Bascom Hall at the top of Bascom Hill, a building that had been around for most of the university's history. The Hall's historic walls didn't accommodate new technology, so the university made certain she had a fancy desk with a built-in screen. The problem with that was that when she did extensive research, as she was doing now, she had to look down. She often downloaded information to her palmtop or worked at home. Working in her office, in the thin light provided by the ancient fluorescents and the dirty meshed window, gave her a headache.

But she was nearly done. Tomorrow, she would take the students from the horrors of trench warfare to the first steps toward U.S. involvement. The bulk of the lecture, though, would focus on isolationism—a potent force in both world wars.

A knock on her door brought her to the 21st century. She rubbed the bridge of her nose impatiently. She wasn't holding office hours. She hated it when students failed to read the signs.

"Yes?" she asked.

"Professor Cross?"

"Yes?"

"May I have a moment of your time?"

The voice was male and didn't sound terribly young, but many of her students were older.

"A moment," she said, using her desktop to unlock the door. "I'm not having office hours."

The knob turned and a man came inside. He wasn't very tall, and he was thin—a runner's build. It wasn't until he turned toward her, though, that she let out a groan.

"Professor Franke."

He held up a hand. "I'm sorry to disturb you—"

"You should be," she said. "I purposely didn't answer your message."

"I figured. Please. Just give me a few moments."

She shook her head. 'I'm not interested in being the subject of any study. I don't have time."

"Is it the time? Or is it the fact that the study has to do with Millennium Babies?" His look was sharp.

"Both."

"I can promise you that you'll be well compensated. And if you'll just listen to me for a moment, you might reconsider—"

"Professor Franke," she said, "I'm not interested."

"But you're a key to the study."

"Why?" she asked. "Because of my mother's lawsuits?"

"Yes," he said.

She felt the air leave her body. She had to remind herself to breathe. The feeling was familiar. It had always been familiar. Whenever anyone talked about Millennium Babies, she had this feeling in her stomach.

Millennium Babies. No one had expected the craze, but it had become apparent by March of 1999. Prospective parents were timing the conception of their children as part of a race to see if their child could be the first born in 2000— the New Millennium, as the pundits of the day inaccurately called it. There was a more-or-less informal international contest, but in the United States, the competition was quite heavy. There were other races in every developed country, and in every city. And in most of those places, the winning parent got a lot of money, and a lot of products, and some, those with the cutest babies, or the pushiest parents, got endorsements as well.

"Oh, goodie," Brooke said, filling her voice with all the sarcasm she muster. "My mother was upset that I didn't get exploited enough as a child so you're here to fill the gap."

His back straightened. "It's not like that."

"Really? How is it then?" She regretted the words the moment she spoke them. She was giving Franke the opening he wanted.

"We've chosen our candidates with care," he said. "We are not taking babies born randomly on January 1 of 2000. We're taking children whose birth was planned, whose parents made public statements about the birth, and whose parents hoped to get a piece of the pie."

"Wonderful," she said. "You're studying children with dysfunctional families."

"Are we?" he asked.

"Well, if you study me, you are," she said and stood. "Now, I'd like it if you leave."

"You haven't let me finish."

"Why should I?"

"Because this study might help you, Professor Cross."

"I'm doing fine without your help."

"But you never talk about your Millennium Baby status."

"And how often do you discuss the day you were born, Professor?"

"My birthday is rather unremarkable," he said. "Unlike yours."

She crossed her arms. "Get out."

"Remember that I study human potential," he said. "And you all have the same beginnings. All of you come from parents who had the same goal—parents who were driven to achieve something unusual."

"Parents who were greedy," she said.

"Some of them," he said. "And some of them planned to have children anyway, and thought it might be fun to try to join the contest."

"I don't see how our beginnings are relevant."

He smiled, and she cursed under her breath. As long as she talked to him, as long as she asked thinly veiled questions, he had her and they both knew it.

"In the past forty years, studies of identical twins raised apart have shown that at least fifty percent of a person's disposition is apparent at birth. Which means that no matter how you're raised, if you were a happy baby, you have a greater than fifty percent chance of being a happy adult. The remaining factors are probably environmental. Are you familiar with DNA mapping?"

"You're not answering my question," she said.

"I'm trying to," he said. "Listen to me for a few moments, and then kick me out of your office."

She wouldn't get rid of him otherwise. She slowly sat in her chair.

"Are you familiar with DNA mapping?" he repeated.

"A little," she said.

"Good." He leaned back in his chair and templed his fingers. "We haven't located a happiness gene or an un-happiness gene. We're not sure what it is about the physical make-up that makes these things work. But we do know that it has something to do with serotonin levels."

"Get to the part about Millennium Babies," she said.

He smiled. "I am. My last book was partly based on the happiness/unhappiness model, but I believe that's too simplistic. Human beings are complex creatures. And as I grow older, I see a lot of lost potential. Some of us were raised to fail, and some were raised to succeed. Some of those raised to succeed have failed, and some who were raised to fail have succeeded. So clearly it isn't all environment."

"Unless some were reacting against their environment," she said, hearing the sullenness in her tone, a sullenness she hadn't used since she last spoke to her mother five years before.

"That's one option," he said, sounding brighter. He must have taken her statement for interest. "But one of the things I learned while working on human potential is that drive is like happiness. Some children are born driven. They walk sooner than others. They learn faster. They adapt faster. They achieve more, from the moment they take their first breath."

"I don't really believe that our entire personalities are formed at birth," she said. "Or that our destinies are written before we're conceived."

"None of us do," he said. "If we did, we wouldn't have a reason to get out of bed in the morning. But we do acknowledge that we're all given traits and talents that are different from each other. Some of us have blue eyes. Some of us can hit golf balls with a power and accuracy that others only dream of. Some of us have perfect pitch, right?"

"Of course," she snapped.

"So it only stands to reason that some of us are born with more happiness than others, and some are born with more drive than others. If you consider those intangibles to be as real as, say, musical talent."

His argument had a certain logic, but she didn't want to agree with him on anything. She wanted him out of her office.

"But," he said. "Those with the most musical talent aren't always the ones on stage at Carnegie hall. There are other factors, environmental factors. A child who grows up without hearing music might never know how to make music, right?"

"I don't know," she said.

"Likewise," he said, "if that musically inclined child had parents to whom music was important, the child might hear music all the time. From the moment that child is born, that child is familiar with music and has an edge on the child who hasn't heard a note."

She started tapping her fingers.

He glanced at them and leaned forward. "As I said in my message, this study focuses on success and failure. To my knowledge, there has never before been a group of children conceived nationwide with the same specific goal in mind."

Her mouth was dry. Her fingers had stopped moving.

"You Millennium Babies share several traits in common. Your parents conceived you at the same time. Your parents had similar goals and desires for you. You came out of the womb and instantly you were branded a success or a failure, at least for this one goal."

"So," she said, keeping her voice cold. "Are you going to deal with all those children who were abandoned by their parents when they discovered they didn't win?"

"Yes," he said.

The quiet sureness of his response startled her. He spread his hands as if in explanation. "Their parents gave up on them," he said. "Right from the start. Those babies are perhaps the purest subjects of the study. They were clearly conceived only with the race in mind."

"And you want me because I'm the most spectacular failure of the group." Her voice was cold, even though she had to clasp her hands together to keep them from trembling.

"I don't consider you a failure, Professor Cross," he said. 'You're well respected in your profession. You're on a tenure track at a prestigious university—"

"I meant as a Millennium Baby. I'm the public failure. When people think of baby contests, the winners never come to mind. I do."

He sighed. "That's part of it. Part of it is your mother's attitude. In some ways, she's the most obsessed parent, at least that we can point to."

Brooke winced.

"I'd like to have you in this study," he said. "The winners will be. It would be nice to have you represented as well."

"So that you can get rich off this book, and I'll be disgraced yet again," she said.

"Maybe," he said. "Or maybe you'll get validated."

Her shoulders were so tight that it hurt to move her head. "'Validated.' Such a nice psychiatrist's word. Making me feel better will salve your conscience while you get rich."

"You seem obsessed with money," he said.

"Shouldn't I be?" she asked. "With my mother?"

He stared at her for a long moment.

Finally, she shook her head. "It's not the money. I just don't want to be exploited any more. For any reason."

He nodded. Then he folded his hands across his stomach and squinched up his face, as if he were thinking. Finally, he said, "Look, here's how it is. I'm a scientist. You're a member of a group that interests me and will be useful in my research. If I were researching thirty-year-old history professors who happened to be on a tenure track, I'd probably interview you as well. Or professional women who lived in Wisconsin. Or—"

"Would you?" she asked. "Would you come to me, really?"

He nodded. "It's policy to check who's available for study at the university before going outside of it."

She sighed. He had a point. "A book on Millennium Babies will sell well. They all do. And you'll get interviews, and you'll become famous."

"The study uses Millennium Babies," he said, "but anything I publish will be about success and failure, not a pop psychology book about people born on January first."

"You can swear to that?" she asked.

"I'll do it in our agreement," he said.

She closed her eyes. She couldn't believe he was talking her into this.

Apparently he didn't think he had, for he continued. "You'll be compensated for your time and your travel expenses. We can't promise a lot, but we do promise that we won't abuse your assistance."

She opened her eyes. That intensity was back in his face. It didn't unnerve her. In fact, it reassured her. She would rather have him passionate about the study than anything else.

"All right," she said. "What do I have to do?"

\*\*\*

FIRST SHE SIGNED WAIVERS. She had all of them checked out by her lawyer—the fact that she even had a lawyer was yet another legacy from her mother—and he said that they were fine, even liberal. Then he tried to talk her out of the study, worried more as a friend, he said, even though he had never been her friend before.

"You've been trying to get away from all of this. Now you're opening it back up? That can't be good for you."

But she wasn't sure what was good for her any more. She had tried not thinking about it. Maybe focusing on herself, on what happened to her from the moment she was born, was better.

She didn't know, and she didn't ask. The final agreement she signed was personalized—it guaranteed her access to her file, a copy of the completed study, and promised that any study her information was used in would concern success and failure only, and would not be marketed as a Millennium Baby product. Her lawyer asked for a few changes, but very few, considering how opposed he was to this project. She was content with the concessions Professor Franke made for her, including the one which allowed her to leave after the first two months.

But the first two months were grueling, in their own way. She had to carve time out of an already full schedule for a complete physical, which included DNA sampling. This had been a major sticking point for her lawyer—that her DNA and her genetic history would not be made available to anyone else—and he had actually gotten Franke to sign forms that attested to that fact. The sampling, for all its trouble, was relatively painless. A few strands of hair, some skin scrapings, and two vials of blood, and she was done.

The psychological exams took the longest. Most of them required the presence of the psychiatric research member of the team, a dour woman who barely spoke to Brooke when she came in. The woman watched while Brook used a computer to take tests: a Rorschach, a Minnesota Multiphasic Personality Interview, a Thematic Apperception Test, and a dozen others whose names she just as quickly forgot. One of them was a standard IQ test. Another was a specialized test designed by Franke's team for his previous experiment. All of them felt like games to Brooke, and all of them took over an hour each to complete.

Her most frustrating time, though, was with the sociologist, a well-meaning man named Meyer. He wanted to correlate her experiences with the experiences of others, and put them in the context of the society at the time. He'd ask questions, though, and she'd correct them—feeling that his knowledge of modern history was poor. Finally she complained to Franke, who smiled, and told her that her perceptions and the researchers' didn't have to match. What was important to them wasn't what was true for the society, but what was true for *her*. She wanted to argue, but it wasn't her study, and she decided she was placing too much energy into all of it.

Through it all, she had weekly appointments with a psychologist who asked her questions she didn't want to think about. *How has being a Millennium Baby influenced your outlook on life? What's your first memory? What do you think of your mother?*

Brooke couldn't answer the first. The second question was easy. Her first memory was of television lights blinding her, creating prisms, and her chubby baby fingers reaching for them, only to be caught and held by her mother's cold hand.

Brooke declined to answer the third question, but

the psychologist asked it at every single meeting. And after every single meeting, Brooke went home and cried.

\*\*\*

SHE GAVE A MID-TERM EXAM in her World Wars class, the first time she had ever done so in a survey class. But she decided to see how effective she was being, since her concentration was more on her own past than the one she was supposed to be teaching.

Her graduate assistants complained about it, especially when they looked at the exam itself. It consisted of a single question: *Write an essay exploring the influences, if any, the First World War had on the Second. If you believe there were no influences, defend that position.*

Her assistants tried to talk her into a simple true/false/multiple choice exam, and she had glared at them. "I don't want to give a test that can be graded by computer," she said. "I want to see a handwritten exam, and I want to know what these kids have learned." And because she wanted to know that—not because of her assistants' complaints (as she made very clear)—she took twenty of the exams to grade herself.

But before she started, she had a meeting in Franke's office. He had called her.

Franke's office was in a part of the campus she didn't get to very often. A winding road took her past Washburn Observatory on a bluff overlooking Lake Mendota, and into a grove of young trees. The parking area was large and filled with small electric and energy efficient cars. She walked up the brick sidewalk. Unlike the sidewalks around the rest of the city, this one didn't have the melting piles of dirty snow that were reminders of the long hard winter. Instead, tulips and irises poked out of the brown dirt lining the walk.

The building was an old Victorian style house, rather large for its day. The only visible signs of a remodel (besides the pristine condition of the paint and roof) were the security system outside, and the heat pump near the driveway.

Clearly this was a faculty-only building; no classes were held here. She turned the authentic glass door knob and stepped into a narrow foyer. A small electronic screen floated in the center of the room. The screen moved toward her.

"I'm here to see Dr. Franke," she said.

"Second floor," the digital voice responded. "He is expecting you."

She sighed softly and mounted the stairs. With the exception of the electronics, everything in the hall reflected the period. Even the stairs weren't covered in carpet, but instead in an old-fashioned runner, tacked on the sides, with a long gold carpet holder pushed against the back of the step.

The stairs ended in a long narrow hallway, illuminated by electric lights done up to resemble gaslights. Only one door stood open. She knocked on it, then, without waiting for an invitation, went in.

The office wasn't like hers. This office was a suite, with a main area and a private room to the side. A leather couch was pushed against the window, and two matching leather chairs flanked it. Teak tables provided the accents, with round gold table lamps the only flourish.

Professor Franke stood in the door to the private area. He looked at her examining his office.

"Impressive," she said.

He shrugged. "The university likes researchers, especially those who add to its prestige."

She knew that. She had published her thesis, and it had received some acclaim in academic circles, which was why she was as far ahead as she was. But very few historians became famous for their research. She doubted she would ever achieve this sort of success.

"Would you like a seat?" Franke asked.

She sat on one of the leather chairs. It was soft, and molded around her. "I didn't think you'd need to interview every subject to see if they wanted to continue," she said.

"Every subject isn't you." He sat across from her. His hair was slightly mussed as if he had been running his fingers through it, and he had a coffee stain above the breast pocket of his white shirt. "We had agreements."

She nodded.

"I will tell you some of what we have learned," he said. "It's preliminary, of course."

"Of course." She sounded calmer than she felt. Her heart was pounding.

"We've found three interesting things. The first is that all Millennium Babies in this study walked earlier than the norm, and spoke earlier as well. Since most were firstborns, this is unusual. Firstborns usually speak *later* than the norm because their every need is catered to. They don't need to speak right away, and when they do, they usually speak in full sentences."

"Meaning?"

"I hesitate to say for certain, but it might be indicative of great drive. Stemming, I believe, from the fact that the parents were driven." His eyes were sparkling. His enthusiasm for his work was catching. She found herself leaning forward like a student in her favorite class. "We're also finding genetic markers in the very areas we were looking for. And some interesting biochemical indications that may help us isolate the biological aspect of this."

"You're moving fast," she said.

He nodded. "That's what's nice about having a good team."

And a lot of subjects, she thought. Not to mention building on earlier research.

"We've also found that there is direct correlation between a child's winning or losing the millennium race and her perception of herself as a success or failure, independent of external evidence."

Her mouth was dry. "Meaning?"

"No matter how successful they are, the majority of Millennium Babies—at least the ones we chose for this study, the ones whose parents conceived them only as part of the race—perceive themselves as failures."

"Including me," she said.

He nodded. The movement was slight, and it was gentle.

"Why?" she asked.

"That's the thing we can only speculate at. At least at this moment." He wasn't telling her everything. But then, the study wasn't done. He tilted his head slightly. "Are you willing to go to phase two of the study?"

"If I say no, will you tell me what else you've discovered?' she asked.

"That's our agreement." He paused and then added, "I would really like it if you continued."

Brooke smiled. "That much is obvious."

He smiled too, and then looked down. "This last part is nothing like the first. You won't have test after test. It's only going to last for a few days. Can you do that?"

Some of the tension left her shoulders. She could do a few days. But that was it. "All right," she said.

"Good." He smiled at her, and she braced herself. There was more. "I'll put you down for the next segment. It doesn't start until Memorial Day. I have to ask you to stay in town, and set aside that weekend."

She had no plans. She usually stayed in town on Memorial Day weekend. Madison emptied out, the students going home, and the city became a small town—one she dearly loved.

She nodded.

He waited a moment, his gaze darting downward, and then meeting hers again. "There's one more thing."

This was why he had called her here. This was why she needed to see him in person.

"I was wondering if your mother ever told you who your father is. It would help our study if we knew something about both parents."

Brooke threaded her hands together willing herself to remain calm. This had been a sensitive issue her entire life. "No," she said. "My mother has no idea who my father is. She went to a sperm bank."

Franke frowned. "I just figured, since your mother seemed so meticulous about everything else, she would have researched your father as well."

"She did," Brooke said. "He was a physicist, very well known, apparently. It was one of those sperm banks that specialized in famous or successful people. And my mother did check that out."

*Your father must not have been as wonderful as they said he was. Look at you. It had to come from somewhere.*

"Do you know the name of the bank?"

"No."

Franke sighed. "I guess we have all that we can, then."

She hated the disapproval in his tone. "Surely others in this study only have one parent."

"Yes," he said. "There's a subset of you. I was just hoping—"

"Anything to make the study complete," she said sarcastically.

"Not anything," he said. "You can trust me on that."

\*\*\*

BROOKE DIDN'T HEAR from Professor Franke again for nearly a month, and then only in the form of a message, delivered to House, giving her the exact times, dates, and places of the Memorial Day meetings. She forgot about the study except when she saw it on her calendar.

The semester was winding down. The mid-term in her World Wars class showed her two things: that she had an affinity for the topic which she was sharing with the students; and that at least two of her graduate assistants had a strong aversion to work. She lectured both assistants, spoke to the chair of the department about teaching the survey class next semester, and continued on with the lectures, focusing on them as if she were the graduate student instead of the professor.

By late April, she had her final exam written—a long cumbersome thing, a mixture of true/false/multiple choice for the assistants, and two essay questions for her. She was thinking of a paper herself—one on the way those wars still echoed through the generations—and she was trying to decide if she wanted the summer to work on it or to teach as she usually did.

The last Saturday in April was unusually balmy, in the seventies without much humidity, promising a beautiful summer ahead. The lilac bush near her kitchen window had bloomed. The birds had returned, and her azaleas were blossoming as well. She was in the garage, digging for a lawn chair that she was convinced she still had when she heard the hum of an electric car.

She came out of the garage, dusty and streaked with grime. A green car pulled into her driveway, next to the ancient pickup she used for hauling.

Something warned her right from the start. A glimpse, perhaps, or a movement. Her stomach flipped over, and she had to swallow sudden nausea. She had left her personal phone inside—it was too nice to be connected to the world today—and she had never gotten the garage hooked into House's computer because she hadn't seen the need for the expense.

Still, as the car shuddered to a stop, she glanced at the screen door, wondering if she could make it in time. But the car's door was already opening, and in this kind of stand-off, fake courage was better than obvious panic.

Her mother stepped out. She was a slender woman. She wore blue jeans and a pale peach summer sweater that accented her silver and gold hair. The hair was new, and had the look of permanence. Apparently her mother had finally decided to settle on a color. She wore gold bangles, and a matching necklace, but her ears were bare.

"I have a restraining order against you," Brooke said, struggling to keep her voice level. "You are not supposed to be here."

"I'm not the one who broke the order." Her mother's voice was smooth and seductive. Her courtroom voice. She had won a lot of cases with that melodious warmth. It didn't seem too strident. It just seemed sure.

"I sure as hell didn't want contact with you," Brooke said.

"No? Is that why your university contacted me?"

Brooke's heart was pounding so hard she wondered if her mother could hear it. "Who contacted you?'

"A Professor Franke, for some study. Something to do with DNA samples. I was to send them through my doctor, but you know I wouldn't do such a thing with anything that delicate."

Son of a bitch. Brooke hadn't known they were going to try something like that. She didn't remember any mention of it, nothing in the forms.

"I have nothing to do with that," Brooke said.

"It seems you're in some study. That seems like involvement to me," her mother said.

"Not the kind that gets you around a restraining order. Now get the hell off my property."

"Brooke, honey," her mother said, taking a step toward her. "I think you and I should discuss this—"

"There's nothing to discuss," Brooke said. "I want you to stay away from me."

"That's silly." Her mother took another step forward. "We should be able to settle this, Brooke. Like adults. I'm your mother—"

"That's not my fault," Brooke snapped. She glanced at the screen door again.

"A restraining order is for people who threaten your life. I've never hurt you, Brooke."

"There's a judge in Dane County who disagrees, Mother."

"Because you were so hysterical," her mother said. "We've had a good run of it, you and I."

Brooke felt the color drain from her face. "How's that, Mother? The family that sues together stays together?"

"Brooke, we have been denied what's rightfully ours. We—"

"It never said in any of those contests that a child had to be born by natural means. You misunderstood, Mother. Or you tried to be even more perfect than anyone else. So what if I'm the first vaginal birth of the new millennium. So what? It was thirty years ago. Let it go."

"The first baby received enough in endorsements to pay for a college education and to have a trust fund—"

"And you've racked up enough in legal fees that you could have done the same." Brooke rubbed her hands over her arms. The day had grown colder.

"No, honey," her mother said in that patronizing tone that Brooke hated. "I handled my own case. There were no fees."

It was like arguing with a wall. "I have made it really, really clear that I never wanted to see you again," Brooke said. "So why do you keep hounding me? You don't even like me."

"Of course I like you, Brooke. You're my daughter."

"I don't like you," Brooke said.

"We're flesh and blood," her mother said softly. "We owe it to each other to be there for each other."

"Maybe you should have remembered that when I was growing up. I was a child, Mother, not a trophy. You saw me as a means to an end, an end you now think you got cheated out of. Sometimes you blame me for that—I was too big, I didn't come out fast enough, I was breach—and sometimes you blame the contest people for not discounting all those 'artificial methods' of birth, but you never, ever blame yourself. For anything."

"Brooke," her mother said, and took another step forward.

Brooke held up her hand. "Did you ever think, Mother, that it's your fault we missed the brass ring? Maybe you should have pushed harder. Maybe you should have had a c-section. Or maybe you shouldn't have gotten pregnant at all."

"Brooke!"

"You weren't fit to be a parent. That's what the judge decided on. You're right. You never hit me. You didn't have to. You told me how worthless I was from the moment I could hear. All that anger you felt about losing you directed at me. Because, until I was born, you never lost anything."

Her mother shook her head slightly. "I never meant that. When I would say that, I meant—"

"See? You're so good at taking credit for anything that goes well, and so bad at taking it when something doesn't."

"I still don't see why you're so angry at me," her mother said.

This time, it was Brooke's turn to take a step forward. "You don't? You don't remember that last official letter? The one cited in my restraining order?"

"You have never understood the difference between a legal argument and the real issues."

"Apparently the judge is just as stupid about legal arguments as I am, Mother." Brooke was shaking. "He believed it when you said that I was brought into this world simply to win that contest, and by rights, the state should be responsible for my care, not you."

"It was a lawsuit, Brooke. I had an argument to make."

"Maybe you can justify it that way, but I can't. I know the truth when I hear it. And so does the rest of the world." Brooke swallowed. Her throat was so tight it hurt. "Now get out of here."

"Brooke, I—"

"I mean it, Mother. Or I will call the police."

"Do you want me at least to do the DNA work?"

"I don't give a damn what you do, so long as I never see you again."

Her mother sighed. "Other children forgive their parents for mistakes they made in raising them."

"Was your attitude a mistake, Mother? Have you re-formed? Or do you still have law suits out there? Are you still trying to collect on a thirty-year-old dream?"

Her mother shook her head and went back to the car. Brooke knew that posture. It meant that Brooke was being unreasonable. Brooke was impossible to argue with. Brooke was the burden.

"Some day," her mother said. "You'll regret how you treated me."

"Why?" Brooke asked. 'You don't seem to regret how you treated me."

"Oh, I regret it, Brooke. If I had known it would have made you so bitter toward me, I never would have talked to you about our problems. I would have handled them alone."

Brooke clenched a fist and then unclenched it. She made herself take a deep breath and, instead of pointing out to her mother that she had done it again—she had blamed Brooke—Brooke said, "I'm calling the police now," and started toward the house.

"There's no need," her mother said. 'I'm going. I'm just sorry—"

And the rest of her words got lost in the bang of the screen door.

\*\*\*

AN HOUR LATER, BROOKE found herself outside Professor Franke's office. She ignored the small electronic screen that floated ahead of her, bleating that she didn't have an appointment and she wasn't welcome in the building. It was a dumb little machine; when she had asked if Professor Franke was in, it had told her he was. A good human secretary would have lied.

Apparently the system had already contacted Franke for he stood in his door, waiting for her, a smile on his face even though his eyes were wary.

"Everything all right, Professor Cross?"

"I never gave you permission to contact my mother," she said as she came up the stairs.

"Your mother?"

"She came to my house today, claiming I'd nullified my restraining order by contacting her. She said you asked her for DNA samples."

"Come into my office," he said.

Brooke walked past him and heard him close the door. "We did contact her, as we did all the parents, for DNA samples. We were explicit in expressing our needs as part of the study, and that they had every right to refuse if they wanted. In no way did we ask her to come here or to tell her that you asked us to contact her."

"She says it came from me and she knew I was involved in the study."

"Of course," he said. "One of the waivers you signed gave us permission to examine your genetic heritage. That includes parents, grandparents, living relatives if necessary. Your attorney didn't object."

Her attorney was good, but not that good. He probably hadn't known what that all entailed.

"I want you to send a letter, through your attorney or the university's counsel, stating that I in no way asked you to contact her and that you did it of your own volition."

"Do you want me to apologize?" he asked.

"To me or to her?" she asked.

He drew in his breath sharply and she realized for the first time that she had knocked him off balance.

"I meant to her," he said, "but I guess I owe you an apology too."

Brooke stared at him for a moment. No one had said that to her before.

"Look," he said, apparently not understanding her silence. "I should have thought it through when your mother said she didn't allow such confidential information to be sent to people she didn't know. I thought that was a refusal."

"For anyone else it would have been," Brooke said. "But not for my mother."

"She's an interesting woman."

"From the outside," Brooke said.

He nodded as if he understood. "For the record, I didn't mean to cause you trouble. I'm sorry I didn't warn you."

"It's all right," Brooke said. "Just don't let it happen again."

\*\*\*

EXCEPT FOR RECEIVING A COPY of the official letter Franke sent to her mother, Brooke didn't think about the study again until Memorial Day weekend. The semester was over. Most of her students successfully answered the question on her World Wars final: *Explain the influence World War I had on World War II.*

One student actually called the World War I the mother of World War II. The phrase stopped Brooke as she read, made her shudder, and hoped that not every monstrous mother begot an even more monstrous child.

Professor Franke sent instructions for Memorial Day weekend with the official letter. He asked her to set aside time from mid-afternoon on Friday to late evening on Monday. She was to report to TheaterPlace, restaurant and bar on the west side of town.

She'd been to the restaurant before. It was a novelty spot in what had once been a fourplex movie palace. The restaurant was in the very center, with huge meeting rooms off to the sides. The builders had called it a gathering place for organizations too small to hold conventions. Still, it had everything—the large restaurant, the bar, places for presentations, places for seminars, places for quiet get-togethers. There were three smaller restaurants in what had once been the projection booths—restaurants that barely seated twenty. One of the larger rooms even showed live theater once a month.

Cars were no longer allowed in this part of town, thanks to a Green referendum three years before. Someone had tried to make exception for electric vehicles but that hadn't worked either as the traffic cops said it would be too hard to patrol. Instead, the light rail made several stops, and some enterprising entrepreneur had built underground tunnels to connect all of the buildings. Many people Brooke knew preferred to shop here in the winter; it kept them out of the freezing cold. But she found the necessity of taking the light rail annoying. She would have preferred her own car so that she could leave on her own schedule.

She walked from the light rail stop near the refurbished mall to TheaterPlace. On the outside, it still looked like a fourplex: the raised roof, the warehouse shape. Only up close did it become apparent that TheaterPlace had been completely gutted and remodeled, right down to the smoke glass that had replaced the clear windows.

A sign on the main entrance notified her that Theater-Place was closed for a private party. She touched the door anyway—knowing the party was theirs—and a scanner instantly identified her.

*Welcome, Brooke Cross. You may enter.*

She shuddered slightly, knowing that Franke had programmed the scanner to recognize either her fingerprints on the backside of the door or her DNA. She felt like her mother, worried that Franke had too much information.

The door clicked open and she let herself inside. A short dark haired woman she had never seen before hurried to her side.

"Professor Cross," the woman said. "Welcome."

"Thanks," Brooke said.

"Just a few rules before we get started," the woman said. "This is the last time we'll be using names today. We ask you not to tell anyone who you are by name, although you may tell them anything else you wish about yourself. Please identify yourself using this number only."

She handed Brooke a stick-on badge with the number 333 printed in bold black numbers.

"Then what?" Brooke asked.

"Wait for Professor Franke to make his announcement. You're in the Indiana Jones room, by the way."

"Thanks," Brooke said. She stuck the label to her white blouse and made her way down the hall. All of the rooms were named after characters from famous movies, and the décor in all of them except the restaurants was the same: movie posters on the wall, soft golden lighting, and a thin light blue carpet. The furniture moved according to the function. She had been in the Jones room before for a faculty party honoring some distinguished professor from Beijing, but she doubted the room would be the same.

The double doors were open and inside, she heard the sound of soft conversation. She stopped just outside the door and surveyed the room.

The lights were up—not soft and golden at all—but full daylight, so that everyone's faces were visible. The Jones room was one of the largest—the only theater, apparently, whose dimensions had been left intact. It seemed about half full.

There were tables lining the wall, with various kinds of foods and beverages, small plates to hold everything, and silverware glimmering in the brightness. People stood in various clusters. There were no chairs, no furniture groupings, and Brooke knew that was on purpose. Small floating serving trays hovered near each group. Whenever someone set an empty glass on one, the tray would float through an opening in the wall, and another tray would take its place.

Something about the groupings made her nervous and it wasn't the lack of chairs or the fact that she didn't know anyone. She stared for a moment, trying to figure out what had caught her.

No one looked the same; they were fat and thin, tall and short. They had long hair and beards, no hair, and dyed hair. They were white, black, Asian and Hispanic or they were multiracial, with no features that marked them as part of any particular ethnic group. They were incredibly diverse—but none of them were elderly or underage. None of them had wrinkles, except for a few laugh lines, and none of them seemed younger than twenty.

They were about the same age. She would guess they *were* the same age—the exact same age as she was. It was a gathering of Franke's subjects for this study: all of them born January 1, 2000. All of them thirty years and 147 days old.

She shuddered. No wonder Franke was worried about this second half of the study. Most studies of this nature didn't allow the participants to get to know each other. She wondered what discipline he was dabbling in now, what sort of results he was expecting.

A man stopped beside her just outside the door. He was wearing a denim shirt, a bolo tie, and tight blue jeans. His long blond hair—naturally sunstreaked—brushed against his collar. He had a tan—something she had rarely seen in her lifetime—and it made his skin a burnished gold. He had letters on his name badge: DKGHY.

"Hi," he said. His voice was deep with a Southern twang. "I guess we just go in, huh?'

"I've been steeling myself for it," she said.

He smiled. "Feels like they took away my armor when they took my name. I'm not sure if I'm supposed to say, 'Hi. I'm DKG—whatever-the-hell the rest of those letters are.' Or if I'm not supposed to say anything at all."

"Well, I don't want to be called 333."

"Can't say as I blame you." He grinned. "How about I call you Tre, and you can call me—oh, hell, I don't know—"

"De," she said. 'I'll call you De."

"Nice to meet you, Tre," he said, holding out his hand.

She took it. His fingers were warm. "Nice to meet you, De."

"Where do y'all hail from?"

"Right here," she said.

"You're kiddin'? No travel expenses, huh?"

"And no hotel rooms."

He grinned. "Sometimes hotel rooms can be nice, especially when you don't get to see the inside of them very often."

"I suppose." She smiled at him. He was making this easier than she expected. "Where're you from?"

"Originally Galveston. But I've been in L'siana a long time now."

"New Orleans?"

"Just outside."

"Some city you got there."

"Yeah, but we ain't got a place like this." He looked around. "Want to go in?"

"Now I do," she said.

They walked side-by-side as if they were a couple who had been together most of their lives. Neither of them looked at the food, although he snatched two bottles of sparkling water off one of the tables, and handed one to her. She opened it, glad to have something to carry.

A few more people came in the doors. She and De went farther into the room. Bits of conversation floated by her:

"…never really got over it…"

"…worked for the past five years as a dental hygienist…"

"…my father wanted to take us out of the country, but…"

Then there was a slight bonging sound, and the conversation halted. Franke stood in the very front of the room, where the theater screen used to be. He was easy to see because the floor slanted downward slightly. He held up his hands, and in a moment there was complete silence.

"I want to thank you all for coming." His voice was being amplified. It sounded as if he were talking right next to Brooke instead of half a room away. "Your assignment today is easy. We do not want you sharing names, but you can talk about anything else. We will be providing meals later on in various restaurants—your badge I.D. will be listed on a door—and we will have drinks in the bar after that. We ask that no one leave before midnight, and that you all return at noon tomorrow for the second phase."

"That's it?" someone asked.

"That's it," Franke said. "Enjoy yourselves."

"I have a bad feeling about this, Tre," De said.

"Me, too," Brooke said. "It can't be this simple."

"I don't think it will be."

She sighed. "Well, we signed on for this, so we may as well enjoy it."

He looked at her sideways, his blue eyes bright. "Want to be my date for the day, darlin'?"

"It's always nice to have one friendly face," she said, surprised at how easily she was flirting with him. She never flirted with anyone.

"That it is." He offered her his arm. "Let's see how many of these nice folks are interested in conversation."

"Mingle, huh?" she asked, as she put her hand in the crook of his arm.

"I think that's what we're meant to do." He frowned. "Only god knows, I 'spect it'll all backfire for the weekend's done."

***

IT DIDN'T BACKFIRE THAT NIGHT. Brooke had a marvelous dinner in one of the small restaurants with De, a woman from Boston, and two men from California. They shared stories about their lives and their jobs, and only touched in passing on the thing that they had in common. In fact, the only time they discussed it was when De brought it up over dessert.

"What made y'all sign up for this foolishness?" he asked.

"The money," said the man from Los Gatos. He was slender to the point of gauntness, with dark eyes and thinning hair. His shirt had wear marks around the collar and was fraying slightly on the cuffs. "I thought it'd be an easy buck. I didn't expect all the tests."

"Me, either," the woman from Boston said. She was tall and broad shouldered, with muscular arms. During the conversation, she mentioned that she had played professional basketball until she was sidelined with a knee injury. "I haven't had so many tests since I got out of school."

The man from Santa Barbara said nothing, which surprised Brooke. He was a short stubby man with more charm than he had originally appeared to have. He had been the most talkative during dinner—regaling them with stories about his various jobs, and his two children.

"How about you, Tre?" De asked Brooke.

"I wouldn't have done it if I wasn't part of the university," she said, and realized that was true. Professor Franke probably wouldn't have had the time to convince her, and she would have dismissed him out of hand.

"Me," De said, "I jumped at it. Never been asked to do something like this before. Felt it was sort of important, you know. Anything to help the human condition."

"You don't really believe that," Santa Barbara said.

"If you don't believe it," Los Gatos said to Santa Barbara, "why'd you sign up?"

"Free flight to Madison, vacationer's paradise," Santa Barbara said, and they all laughed. But he never did answer the question.

***

WHEN BROOKE GOT HOME, she sat on her porch and looked at the stars. The night was warm. The crickets were chirping and she thought she heard a frog answer them from a nearby ditch.

The evening had disturbed her in its simplicity. Like everyone else, she wanted to know what Franke was looking for. The rest of the study had been so directed, and this had been so free form.

Dinner had been nice. Drinks afterward with a different group had been nice as well. But the conversation rarely got deeper than anecdotes and current history. No one discussed the study, and no one discussed the past.

She lost De after dinner, which gave her a chance to meet several other people: a woman from Chicago, twins from Akron, and three friends from Salt Lake City. She'd had a good time, and found people she could converse with—one historian, two history buffs, and a librarian who seemed to know a little bit about everything.

De joined her later in the evening, and walked her to the rail stop. He'd leaned against the plastic shelter and smiled at her. She hadn't met a man as attractive as he was in a long time. Not since college.

"I'd ask you to my hotel," he said, "but I have a feelin' anything we do this weekend, in or out of that strange building, is going to be fodder for scientists."

She smiled. She'd had that feeling too.

"Still," he said, "I got to do one thing."

He leaned in and kissed her. She froze for a moment; she hadn't been kissed in nearly ten years. Then she eased into it, putting her arms around his neck and kissing him back, not wanting to stop, even when he pulled away.

"Hmm," he said. His eyes were closed. He opened them slowly. "I think that's titillatin' enough for the scientists, don't you?"

She almost said no. But she knew better. She didn't want to read about her sex life in Franke's next book.

The rail came down the tracks, gliding silently toward them. "See you tomorrow?" she asked.

"You can bet on it," De said. And there had been promise in his words, promise she wasn't sure she wanted to hear.

She brought her knees onto her lawn chair, and wrapped her arms around them. Part of her wished he was here, and part of her was glad he wasn't. She never let anyone come to her house. She didn't want to share it. She had had enough invasions of privacy in her life to prevent this one.

But she had nearly invited De, a man she didn't really know. Maybe De really wasn't a Millennium Baby. Perhaps a bunch of people weren't. Perhaps that was what the numbers and the letters meant. She had spent much of the evening staring at them, wondering. They appeared to be randomly generated, but that couldn't be. They had to have some purpose.

She shook her head and rested her cheek on her knees. She was taking this much too seriously, like she always took things. And soon she would be done with it. She would have bits of information she hadn't had before, and she would store them into a file in her mind, never to be examined again.

Somehow that thought made her sad. The night was beginning to get chilly. She stood, stretched, and made her way to bed.

\*\*\*

THE NEXT MORNING, they met in a different room—the Rose room—named after the character in the 20th century movie *Titanic*. Brooke hoped that the name wasn't a sign.

There were pastries and coffee against the wall, along with every kind of juice imaginable and lots of fresh fruit, but again, there were no chairs. Brooke's feet hurt from the day before—she usually stood to lecture, but not for several hours—and she hoped she'd get a chance to sit before the day was out.

She was nearly late again, and hurried inside as they closed the doors. The room smelled of fresh air mixed with coffee and sweat. The group had gathered again, the faces vaguely familiar now, even the faces of people she hadn't yet met. The people toward the back who saw her enter, smiled at her or nodded in recognition. It felt like they had all bonded simply by spending an evening in the same room. An evening and the promise of a long weekend.

She shivered. The air-conditioning was on high, and the room was cold. It would warm up before the day was out; the sheer number of bodies guaranteed that. But she still wondered if she was dressed warmly enough in her casual lilac blouse and her khaki pants.

"Strange how these places look the same, day or night."

She turned. De was half a step behind her, his long hair loose about his face. He still wore jeans and his fancy boots, but instead of the denim shirt and bolo tie, he wore an understated white open collar shirt that accented his tan. Somehow, she suspected, he seemed more comfortable in this. Had he worn the other as a way of identifying himself or a way of putting others off? She would probably never know.

"The people look different," she said.

"Just a little." He smiled at her. "You look nice."

"And you're flirting."

He shrugged. "I always believe in using my time wisely."

She smiled, and turned as a hush fell over the crowd. Franke had mounted the stage in front. He seemed very small in this place. A few of his assistants stood on either side of him.

"Here it comes," De said.

"What?"

"Whatever it is that's going to make this cocktail party stop." He was staring at Franke too, and his clear blue eyes seemed wary. "I've half a mind to leave now. Want to join me?"

"And do what?"

"Dunno. See the sights?"

It sounded like a good idea. But, as she had said the day before, she had signed up for this, and she didn't break her commitments. And, she had to admit, she was curious.

She bit her lower lip, trying to think of a good way to respond. Apparently she didn't have to.

De sighed. "Didn't think so."

The silence in the room was growing. Franke stared at all of them, rocking slightly on his feet. If Brooke had to guess, she would have thought him very nervous.

"All right," he said. "I have a few announcements. First, we will be serving lunch at 1 p.m. in the main restaurant. Dinner will be at 7 in the same place. You will not have assigned seating. Secondly, after I'm through, you're free to tell each other your names. We've had enough of secrets."

He paused, and this time Brooke felt it, that dread she had seen in De's eyes.

"Finally, I would like everyone with a letter on your name badge to go to the right side of the room, and everyone with a number to go to the left."

People stood for a moment, looking around, waiting for someone to go first. De put a hand on her shoulder. "Here goes nothing," he said. He ran his finger along her collarbone and then walked to the right.

"Come on, folks," Franke said. "It's not hard. Letters to the right. Numbers to the left."

Brooke could still feel De's hand on her skin. She looked in his direction, seeing his blond head towering over the small group of letters who had gathered near the pastries on the far right wall.

She took a deep breath and headed left.

The numbers had gathered near the pastries too, only on the left. She wondered what Franke's researchers would make of that. Los Gatos was there, his hand hovering between the cinnamon rolls and the donuts as if he couldn't decide. So was one of the twins from Akron, and the woman from Boston. Brooke joined them.

"What do you think this is?" Brooke asked.

"A way of identifying us as we run through the maze."

Brooke recognized that voice. She turned and saw Santa Barbara. He shrugged and smiled at her.

She picked up a donut hole and ate it, then made herself a cup of tea while she waited for the room to settle.

It finally did. There was an empty space in the center of the carpet, a space so wide it seemed like an ocean to her.

"Good," Franke said. "Now I'm going to tell you what the badges mean."

There was a slight murmuring as the groups took that in. Boston, Santa Barbara, and Los Gatos flanked Brooke. Her dinner group, minus De.

"Those of you with letters are real Millennium Babies."

Brooke felt a protest rise in her throat. She was born on January 1, 2000. She was a Millennium Baby.

"You were all chosen as such by your state or your country or your city. Your parents received endorsements or awards or newspaper coverage. Those of you with numbers…"

"Are fucking losers," Los Gatos mumbled under his breath.

"…were born near midnight on January 1, but were too late to receive any prizes. You're here because your parents also received publicity or gave interviews before you were born stating that the purpose behind the pregnancy wasn't to conceive a child, but to conceive a child born a few seconds after midnight on January 1 of 2000. You were created to be official Millennium Babies, and failed to receive that title."

Franke paused briefly.

"So, feel free to make real introductions, and mingle. The facility is yours for the day. All we ask is that you do not leave until we tell you to."

"That's it?" Boston asked.

"That's enough," Santa Barbara said. "He's just turned us into the haves and the have-nots."

"Son of a bitch," Los Gatos said.

"We knew that the winners were here," Boston said.

"Yeah, but I assumed there'd be only a few of them," Los Gatos said. "Not half the group."

"It makes sense though," Santa Barbara said. "This is a study of success and failure."

Brooke listened to them idly. She was staring at the right side of the room. All her life, she had been programmed to hate those people. She even studied a few of them, looking them up on the net, seeing how many articles were written about them.

She had stopped when she was ten. Her mother had caught her, and told her what happened to the others didn't matter. Brooke and her mother would have made more of the opportunity, if they had just been given their due.

Their due.

De was staring at her from across the empty carpet. That look of dread was still on his face.

"So," Santa Barbara said. "I guess we can use real names now."

"I guess," said Los Gatos. He hitched up his pants, and glanced at Boston.

She shrugged. "I'm Julie Hunt. I was born at 12:15 Eastern Standard Time in…"

Brooke stopped listening. She didn't want to know about the failures. She knew how it felt to be part of their group. But she didn't know what it was like to be with the winners.

She wiped her damp hands on her pants and crossed the empty carpet. De watched her come. In fact the entire room watched her passage as if she were Moses parting the Red Sea.

The successes weren't talking to each other. They were staring at her.

When she was a few feet away from him, he reached out and pulled her to his side, as if she were in some sort of danger and he needed to recognize her.

"Comin' to the enemy?" he asked, and there was some amusement in his tone. "Or'd they give you a number when you shoulda had a letter?"

The lie would have been so easy. But then she would have had to lie about everything, and that wouldn't work. "No," she said. "I was born at 12:05 a.m. in Detroit, Michigan."

One of the women toward the back looked at her sharply. Anyone from Michigan might recognize that time. Her mother's lawsuits created more than enough publicity. Out of the corner of her eye, Brooke saw Franke. She could feel his intensity meters away.

"Then how come you made the crossin', darlin'?" De's accent got thicker when he was nervous. She had never noticed that before.

She could have given him the easy answer, that she wanted to be beside him, but it wasn't right. The way the entire group was staring at her, eyes wide, lips slightly parted, breathing shallow. It was as if they were afraid she was going to do something to them. But what could she do? Yell at them for something that was no fault of their own? They were the lucky ones. They'd been born at the right time in the right place.

But because they hadn't earned that luck, they were afraid of her. After all, she had been part of the same contest. Only she had been a few minutes late.

No one had moved. They were waiting for her to respond.

"I guess I came," she said, "because I wanted to know what it was like to be a winner."

"Standing over here won't make you a winner," one of the men said.

She flushed. "I know that. I came to listen to you. To see how you've lived. If that's all right."

"I'm not sure I understand you, darlin'," De said. Only his name wasn't De. She didn't know his name. Maybe she never would.

"You were all born winners. From the first moment. Just like we were losers."

Her voice carried in the large room. She hadn't expected the acoustics to be so good.

"I don't know about everyone else in my group, but my birth time has affected my entire life. My mother—" Brooke paused. She hadn't meant to discuss her mother "—never let me forget who I was. And I was wondering if any of you experienced that. Or if you felt special because you'd won. Or if you even knew."

Her voice trailed off at the end. She couldn't imagine not knowing. A life of blissful ignorance. If she hadn't known, she might have gone on to great things. She might have reached farther, tried harder. She might have expected success with every endeavor, instead of being surprised at it.

They were staring at her as if she were speaking Greek. Maybe she was.

"I don't know why it matters," a man said beside her. "It was just a silly little contest."

"I hadn't even remembered it," a woman said, "until Dr. Franke's people contacted me."

Brooke felt something catch in her throat. "Was it like that for all of you?"

"Of course not," De said. "I got interviewed every New Year's like clockwork. What's it like five years into the millennium? Ten? Twenty? That's one of the reasons I moved to L'siana. I'm not much for attention, 'specially the kind I don't deserve."

"Money was nice," one of the women said. "It got me to college."

Another woman shook her head. "My folks spent it all."

More people from the left were moving across the divide, as if they were drawn to the conversation.

"So'd mine," said one of the men.

"There wasn't any money with mine. Just got my picture in the newspaper. Still have that on my wall," another man said.

Brooke felt someone bump her from behind. Los Gatos had joined her. So had Santa Barbara and Boston—um, Julie.

"Why'd this contest make such a difference to you?" one of the letter women asked. She was staring at Brooke.

"It didn't," Brooke said after a moment. "It mattered to my mother. She lost."

"Hell," De said. "People lose. That's part of living."

Brooke looked at him. There was a slight frown mark between his eyes. He didn't understand either. He didn't know what it was like being outside, with his face pressed against the glass.

"Three weeks after I was born," Los Gatos said, "My parents dumped me with a friend of theirs, saying they weren't ready for a baby. I never saw them. I don't even know what they look like."

"My parents said they couldn't afford me," Santa Barbara said. "They were planning on some prize money."

"They abandoned you too?" the woman asked.

"No," he said. "They just made it clear they didn't appreciate the financial burden. If they'd won, I wouldn't've been a problem."

"Sure you would have," De said. "They just would've blamed their problems on something else."

"It's not that simple," Brooke said. Her entire body was sweating despite the chill in the room. "It was a contest, a race. A lot of people didn't look beyond that. There were news articles about abandoned and abused babies, and there were a disproportionate number born in December, January, and February of 2000, because parents wanted to split some of the glory."

"You can't tell me," De said, "that something as insignificant as the time we were born determines our future."

"It does," Brooke said, "if we're brought up to believe it does."

"That bear out, Professor Franke?" De said.

Brooke turned. The professor was standing close to them, listening, looking both bemused and perplexed. Apparently he had expected some kind of reaction, but probably not this one.

"That's what I'm trying to determine," Franke said.

"And I'm askin' you if you determined it," De said.

Franke glanced at one of his assistants. The assistant shrugged. The entire room full of people was crowded around Franke, and was silent for the second time that day.

"This part of the study is experimental," he said. "I'm not sure if answering you will corrupt it."

"But you want to answer me," De said.

Franke smiled. "Yes, I do."

"It's an experiment," Brooke said. "You can always throw this part out. You might have done that anyway. Isn't that what you told me? Or at least implied?"

Franke glanced from her to De. Then Franke straightened his shoulders, as if the gesture made him stronger. "I believe that Brooke is right. My studies have convinced me that something becomes important to a child's development because that child is told that something is important."

"So us losers will remain losers the rest of our lives," Los Gatos said.

Franke shook his head. "That is not my conclusion. I believe that when something becomes important, you chose how to react to it." His voice got louder as he spoke. His professor's voice. "Some of you wearing letters have not done as well as expected. You've rebelled against those expectations and worked at proving you are not as good as you were told you were."

A flush colored De's tan cheeks.

"Others lived up to the expectations and a few of you, a very small few, exceeded them. But—" Franke paused dramatically. "Those of you who wear numbers are financially more successful as a group than your lettered peers. You strive harder because you feel you have something to overcome."

Brooke felt Los Gatos shift behind her.

"I think it goes back to the parameters of the study," Franke said. "Your parents—all of your parents—wanted to improve their lot. They all had drive, therefore most of you have drive. We've found a biological correlation."

"Really? Wow," Santa Barbara said.

"But there's more than biology at work here."

"I'd hope so," De said. "I'd hate to think you can determine who I am by reading my genes."

Franke gave him a small smile. "Your parents," Franke said, "all chose a contest as the method of improving their lives. A lottery, if you will. And most of them failed to win. Or if they succeeded, they discovered Easy Street wasn't so easy after all. You numbered folk have realized that luck is overrated. The only thing you can trust is work you do yourselves."

"And what about those of us with letters?" one of the twins from Akron asked.

"You learned a different lesson. Most of you learned that luck is what you make of it. You might win the lottery, but that doesn't make you or your family any happier than before." Franke looked at Brooke. "There were a lot of studies, some of them prompted by your mother, that showed how many unsuccessful Millennium Babies were abandoned or mistreated. But the successful ones had similar problems. Only no one wanted to lose the golden goose as long as it was still golden. Many of those abandonments were emotional, not physical. People became parents to become rich or famous, not because they wanted children."

"Sounds like you should be studying our parents," Los Gatos said.

Franke grinned. "Now you have my next book."

And the group laughed.

"Feel free to enjoy the rest of the day," Franke said. "Over the rest of the weekend, I'll be talking to individuals among you, wrapping things up. I want to thank you for your time and participation."

"That's it?" De asked.

"When you leave here tonight, if I haven't spoken to you," Franke said, "that's it."

His words were met with a momentary silence. Then he started to make his way through the group. Some people stopped him. Brooke didn't. She turned away, not sure how to feel.

She wasn't as successful as she wanted to be, but she was better off than her mother had said she would be. Brooke had her own house, a good job, interests that meant something to her.

But she was as alone as her mother was. In that, at least, they were the same.

"So," De said. "Is your life profoundly different thanks to this study?"

The question had a mixed tone. Half sarcasm, half serious. He seemed to be waiting for her answer.

"What's your name?" she asked.

"Adam," he said, wincing. "Adam Lassiter."

"The first man."

"If I'd missed my birth time, I'd have been named Zeb." He smiled as he said that, but his eyes didn't twinkle.

"I'm Brooke Cross." She waited, wondering if he'd guess at the name, despite the change. He didn't. Or if he did, he didn't say anything.

"You didn't answer my question," he said.

She looked at the room, at all the people in it, most engaged in private conversations now, hands moving, gazes serious as they compared and contrasted their experiences, trying to see if they agreed with Professor Franke.

"When I was a little girl," she said. "We lived in a small white house, maybe 1200 square feet. A starter, my mother called it, because that was all she could afford. And to me, that house was the world. My mother's world."

"What kind of world was that?" he asked.

She shook her head. How to explain it? But he had asked, and she had to try.

"A world where she did everything right and failed, and everyone else cheated and somehow succeeded. If she'd had the same kind of breaks your parents had, she believed she would have done better than they did. If she hadn't had a child like me, one who was chronically late, her life would have been better."

He was watching her. The crease between his eyes grew deeper.

Her heart was pounding, but she made herself continue. "A few years ago, when I was looking for my own home, I saw dozens and dozens of houses, and somewhere I realized that to the people living in them, those houses were the world."

"So each block has dozens of tiny worlds," he said.

She smiled at him. "Yeah."

"I still don't see how that relates."

She looked at him, then at the room. The other conversations were continuing, as serious as hers was with him. "You asked me if this study changed my life. I can't answer that. I can say, though, that it made me realize one thing."

His gaze was as intense as Franke's.

"It made me realize that even though I had moved out of that house, I hadn't left my mother's world."

He studied her for a moment longer, then said, "Sounds like a hell of a realization."

"Maybe," she said. "It depends on what I do with it."

He laughed. "Thus proving Franke's point."

She flushed. She hadn't realized she had done so, but she had. He leaned toward her.

"You know, Brooke," Adam said softly, "I like women who are chronically late. It balances my habitual timeliness. How's about we have lunch and talk about our histories. Not just the day we were born, but other things, like what we do and where we live and who we are."

She almost refused. He was from Louisiana, and she was from Wisconsin. This friendship—if that's all it was—could go nowhere.

But it was that attitude which had limited her all along. She had been driven, as Franke said, to succeed materially and professionally on her own merits. But she had never tried to succeed socially.

She had never wanted to before.

"And," she said, "you get to tell me what you learned from this study."

"Assumin," he said with a grin, "that I'm the kinda man who can learn anything a'tall."

"Assuming that," she said and slipped her hand in his. It felt good to touch someone else, even if it was only for a brief time. It felt good.

It felt different.

It felt right.

# About the Author

INTERNATIONAL BESTSELLING WRITER Kristine Kathryn Rusch has published fiction in every genre. She has been nominated for three Edgar Awards, two Shamus Awards, and an Anthony Award. She has won the *Ellery Queen* Reader's Choice Award twice. She has also won two Hugo awards, a World Fantasy Award, and three *Asimov's* Readers Choice Awards. She writes mystery as Kris Nelscott, paranormal romance as Kristine Grayson, as well as the science fiction and fantasy that she's known for under Rusch. For more information about her work, please go to kristinekathrynrusch.com.

## Also by
# Kristine Kathryn Rusch

### The Retrieval Artist Series:

*The Disappeared*
*Extremes*
*Consequences*
*Buried Deep*
*Paloma*
*Recovery Man*
*Duplicate Effort*
*Anniversary Day*
*Blowback*

### The Smokey Dalton Series (as Kris Nelscott):

*A Dangerous Road*
*Smoke-Filled Rooms*
*Thin Walls*
*Stone Cribs*
*War at Home*
*Days of Rage*

wMG
Publishing

www.ingramcontent.com/pod-product-compliance
Lightning Source LLC
Chambersburg PA
CBHW052138170626
46812CB00004B/1481